Tall Tales

A 1959 Selection of the
WEEKLY READER
Children's Book Club
EDUCATION CENTER, COLUMBUS 16, OHIO

Tall Tales of America

BY IRWIN SHAPIRO

ILLUSTRATED BY AL SCHMIDT

GUILD PRESS, INC.

POUGHKEEPSIE, NEW YORK

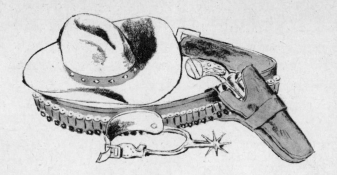

Pecos Bill

ALL cowboys are humans, no matter what they try to tell you. That goes for Pecos Bill, too—and he was the greatest cowboy that ever was.

Bill had to be great to do what he did. He was the first man to throw a lariat. He taught the broncos to buck. He made up a hundred and one cowboy songs. He just about invented the whole cow business single-handed.

Bill did think he was a coyote for a while, instead of a human. You see, he hailed from east Texas, which isn't a bad place for a cowhand to hail from. Exactly where he was born, though, Bill never knew. He couldn't be blamed. He was only a baby at the time.

Anyway, when Bill was a couple of days old, he got some neighbors. Another family settled down about fifty miles away. Bill's Pa didn't like it a bit.

"The country around here is gittin' too crowded," Bill's Pa said to Bill's Ma. "I'm a man that needs elbow room. We'll have to move."

It didn't take Bill's Pa and Ma long to get started. They packed all their belongings in a wagon. On top of the belongings, Bill and his seventeen brothers and sisters piled in.

"Ready? Let's go!" said Bill's Pa, and they headed west.

After they had crossed the Pecos River, one of the wagon wheels hit a rock. Bill was sitting on the tailpiece, and whump! off he went. He landed on his head, so he wasn't hurt much. But he did have the breath knocked out of him. And while he sat on the ground catching his breath, the wagon rolled on.

With seventeen other children on the wagon, Bill's folks didn't miss him for several days. They turned back and searched for him, but it was too late. They couldn't find hide nor hair of Bill.

"Too bad," said Bill's Pa. "I kind of liked the little shaver. But he'll get along. The boy knows how to take care of himself."

Bill's Pa was right. Bill met up with a pack of coyotes, and they got along just fine. Bill settled down with the coyotes and learned coyote talk. He hunted with them by day, and howled at the moon with them by night. Growing up with the coyotes that way, Bill naturally thought he was a coyote himself. He couldn't be blamed. Anybody else would have thought the same.

Bill might never have known he was a human, if a cowboy hadn't come riding up to him one day. Bill was chomping on a cactus, eating his breakfast.

"Boy, howdy," said the cowboy.

Bill only grunted, and kept chomping away.

"If you don't mind my askin'," said the cowboy, "how come you're runnin' around with the varmints?"

Bill threw the cowboy a look that would have dropped a steer.

"Who else would I be runnin' around with?" he said. "I'm a varmint myself. If you'd open your eyes more, and your mouth less, you'd see I'm a coyote."

"No such thing," the cowboy said. "You're a human. Or leastways, a Texan."

"You must be plumb loco, stranger. Ain't I ornery like a coyote?"

The cowboy shook his head. "Don't mean a thing. Lots of Texans is ornery."

"Maybe. But don't I howl at night like a coyote?"

"Most Texans howl," said the cowboy. "And if you're a sure-enough coyote, where's your tail?"

Bill turned his head and whirled around, trying to see if he had a tail.

"Well, tan my hide!" he said. "No tail a-tall! I must be a human. How come the coyotes never told me?"

"Guess they never noticed. Or maybe they were too polite to say," the cowboy said.

Now that he knew he was a human, Bill had to give up living with the coyotes. So he decided to become a cowboy, which was the next best thing.

"Pardner," he said, "I'm kind of new to human doin's. I'd be obliged if you sort of got me started."

"Can do," the cowboy said.

The two of them went to town, where the cowboy staked Bill to some clothes and a horse.

"Now what?" asked Bill.

"Get yourself a job," said the cowboy. "I hear the IXL Ranch could use a good hand."

"Much obliged," Bill said.

Jumping on his horse, he rode off toward the IXL Ranch. He'd been riding for an hour or so, when his horse stumbled and broke a leg. Bill had to shoot the poor critter to put it out of its misery. He picked up his saddle and went on by foot.

Now if there's anything a cowboy hates, that's walking. It was even worse for Bill. He'd never worn shoes before, let alone high-heeled, narrow-toed cowboy boots. What with his boots pinching, and the saddle hanging heavy on his shoulder, Bill was plenty grouchy.

"A million miles from nowhere, and no hoss," he said. "There's more to bein' a human than I thought. Don't know that I care for it."

Just then a big rattlesnake, ten feet long or more, reared up in front of him. It was full of poison, and spoiling for a fight—which was all right with Bill.

"I give you fair warnin'," he said. "I'm a human, but I was raised a coyote. Pizen or no pizen, you don't stand a chance."

The rattler rattled and stuck out its forked tongue.

"All right! You asked for it, you ornery sidewinder!" said Bill.

Just to even things up, he gave the rattler the first three bites. Then he got a good grip on the varmint, shaking it so hard its rattles dropped off. The rattler was so ashamed it just gave up.

"Oh, well! Half a fight's better than none," Bill said.

Feeling some better, he started walking again. He carried his saddle on one shoulder, the rattler over the other. Once in a while he'd give the rattler a twirl through the air. It was fun for the rattler and helped Bill pass the time. Twirling the rattler gave Bill the idea for the lariat—but that came later. Right now there was more trouble ahead.

The trouble was a big wouser, which was the most terrible critter in the West. It was a bit like a mountain lion, a bit like a grizzly bear—and worse than either or both. The wouser was crouching on the rocky wall of a canyon. As Bill walked by, the wouser leaped. Bill ducked, and the wouser missed him. It landed hard on the ground, which didn't sweeten its temper a bit.

"Wou!" said the wouser.

"Looks like I got another fight on my hands," said Bill. "Things are pickin' up!"

Bill lit into the wouser, and he really made the fur

fly. There was so much fur flying that it darkened the sky over all Texas. Many a cowhand rolled up in his blanket, thinking the night had come. But it was only Bill battling the wouser.

It was quite a fracas, at that. Blinded by its own flying fur, the wouser went for Bill with tooth and claw. The sky grew darker and darker, and out of the darkness came Bill's voice:

"I'll make you say uncle, or my name's not Pecos Bill."

Right on top of that, there was a roaring and a screeching and a howling. It might have been the wouser, or it might have been Bill. Anyway, it went on for a spell. Then the fur sort of blew away, and the sun shone again. The wouser was stretched out on the ground. Bill was standing with one foot on the wouser and humming a little tune.

"Wou!" said the wouser, looking up at Bill.

Bill folded his arms and went on humming his tune. But he didn't take his foot off the wouser.

"Uncle," said the wouser.

"That's better," said Bill. "And seein' as how I've got no hoss, I might as well ride you."

He cinched his saddle on the wouser and jumped on. Riding along, he threw loops with the rattler. He had lost his grouch and was feeling fine. He started whooping and yelling, almost as if he was still a coyote.

He was still whooping it up and twirling the rattler when he got to the IXL Ranch. The cowboys were sitting around the chuckwagon, eating bacon and beans. They took a look at Bill, and their tin plates dropped out of their hands.

"Who's the boss of this outfit?" asked Bill.

One long, tall galoot of a cowboy stood up. He had a face that would have stopped a ten-dollar clock. He wore two guns and had a couple of bowie knives stuck in his belt.

"Stranger," he said, "I was. But not never no more. You're boss, beginnin' now."

"That makes sense," Bill said. "High Pockets, you can be my top hand. And the first thing you do is git me a hoss. I don't mind ridin' a wouser once in a while, but I wouldn't want to make it a habit. They're built too close to the ground, and my feet drag."

"Sure thing," said High Pockets. "I'll ride into town and get you the best hoss money can buy."

Bill shook his head. "Nope. Them store-bought hosses is too puny. Why not go out on the range and git me a wild mustang?"

"It's never been done," the cowboys said. "All cowboys buy their hosses in town."

"It's goin' to be done now. Come on, I'll show you how," Bill said.

Slapping the wouser, Bill rode out to the range. The cowboys followed him. As soon as they came to a herd of wild mustangs, Bill ripped his saddle off the wouser.

He threw it over one of the mustangs and hopped on. The horse just stood, waiting for orders from Bill.

"What ails this bronc? Why won't she buck?" Bill asked.

The cowboys had never heard of bucking, and the bronc likewise. Then and there, Bill taught the horses to buck. He taught them rearing, side-winding, back-flipping, sun-fishing, and lots more. Before long he was riding a bucking bronco, fanning its ears with his hat.

"Don't just stand there with your bare faces hangin' out!" Bill called to the cowboys. "Yell! Whoop it up!"

"Don't know any yells," they said.

Bill showed them how to whoop it up, and soon they were yelling: "Yipee! Whoopie! Ride 'em, cowboy!

Yipee!" And cowboys have been yelling like that ever since.

Bill's horse was a smart one. It learned to buck so well that it threw him. Bill couldn't be blamed. He'd never been on a horse before, let alone on a bucking bronco.

"Better forgit about this here buckin'," the cowboys said. "It looks pretty, but it won't work."

Bill picked himself up, dusting off his pants.

"There ain't a man that can't be throwed, there ain't a hoss that can't be rode," he said. "Remember that."

That was the first time, and the last time, a horse ever threw Bill. Bucking spread all over the West, becoming a regular part of the cow business.

"From now on," Bill said, "any of you waddies wants a hoss, you catch a wild bronco and bust him. Savvy?"

"We savvy, Bill," said the cowboys.

"All right then," Bill said. "Now lead me to those steers, and let's start workin' them cattle."

As they rode away, the cowboys started singing. The song was some kind of foolishness about being buried in the deep blue sea.

"Quiet!" roared Bill, sudden-like, firing his pistols into the air.

And all was quiet. Nothing could be heard but the jingling of spurs, from the cowboys shivering in their saddles.

At last High Pockets asked, "Wh-what's the matter, Bill? Don't you care for singin'?"

"It ain't that," said Bill. "I can stand the noise if you can. But it makes my blood boil, hearin' you warble a sea-goin' ditty. You're cowboys, and you ought to sing cowboy songs."

"What cowboy songs?" said the cowboys.

It seems that there weren't any. They just hadn't been

invented yet. But Bill took care of that, and pronto. Right then and there he made up new words to the song the cowboys had been singing. Soon they were all roaring:

> *Oh, bury me not on the lone prairie,*
> *Where the wild coyote will howl o'er me.*
> *In a narrow grave just six by three,*
> *Oh, bury me not on the lone prairie.*

Riding along, Bill made up more songs, such as *The Cowboy's Lament, The Chisholm Trail,* and plenty more.

When he got to where the cattle were roaming the range, he said:

"Let's get down to cases and start workin' these cows. A couple of you cowpokes start ridin' herd, while me and High Pockets git set for a roundup."

The cowboys had never heard of riding herd, or roundups, or any of those things. Most of the time, they just let the cows roam the range. When they wanted to catch one, they would set a trap. A cowboy would hide behind a bush or a rock, and throw a loop of rope on the ground. By and by a cow would come along and step into the loop. Pulling the rope tight, the cowboy would lead the cow away.

"Takes a little time, but we catch a lot of 'em that way," High Pockets said. "I don't mean to brag, but once I caught two cows in the same week. I admit that's a mite unusual. One cow a week is more like it."

That really got Bill riled up. He'd made up songs for herding and roundups, and he didn't want them going to waste. So he changed the cow business to fit the songs. The first thing he did was invent the lariat. He got the idea from twirling that rattler. He made a lariat for himself out of rawhide. It was as long as the equator, except for one end, which was two feet shorter.

After that, Bill taught the cowboys to lasso the steers. He taught them riding herd, branding and roundups, with all the fixings.

Bill himself was a great hand at lassoing. He could lasso a whole herd of cattle at one time, and once he lassoed a cyclone that was passing by. Bill hopped on it, riding it like a bronco. He fanned that old cyclone with his hat, meanwhile kicking a streak of lightning out of his way. The cyclone reared and bucked, trying to throw Bill. It couldn't, of course, so it rained out from under him. Bill hit the ground so hard he drove it down a hundred feet below sea level. He called the place Death Valley, and it's still there. So is the place where Bill's hip pockets made a mark in the rock.

By this time, Bill had the IXL Ranch running the way he wanted. And he had him a horse that he really liked. Bill named it Widow Maker, and wouldn't ever let anybody else ride it. Too dangerous.

It was on account of Widow Maker that Bill lost Slue Foot Sue. Bill happened to be near the Rio Grande one day, when he heard a whooping and a hollering. He turned around to see what was raising such a ruckus, and there was a girl riding a catfish up the river. Now a full-grown Texas catfish is about the size of an ordinary whale, but the girl wasn't having a bit of trouble. She kept riding along, singing and yelling, with her red hair streaming in the breeze.

Bill and the girl took a long look at each other. It was love at first sight.

"Howdy," said the girl. "My name's Slue Foot Sue. What's your handle?"

"Howdy, ma'am. I'm Pecos Bill," said Bill.

Bill had never seen a girl like Sue before, and he knew he'd never see another. He started courting her then and there.

"I don't mean to be forward, ma'am," he said. "But how about you and me gittin' hitched?"

Slue Foot Sue giggled.

"Sure thing, Bill," she said. "I was wonderin' when you'd ask."

Bill and Sue went back to the ranch, where they got ready for the wedding. Everything was fine, except for Sue wanting to ride Widow Maker.

"I'd do anything in the world for you, Sue," said Bill. "But not that. Nobody can ride that hoss except me. He's too ornery."

The day of their wedding, though, Sue asked Bill again. She was wearing her wedding dress and looked as pretty as a picture. Bill just had to say yes. He couldn't be blamed. Any bridegroom would have done the same.

"Yipee!" yelled Sue, getting on Widow Maker.

She didn't stay there long. The horse bucked, sending Sue flying up into the air. The trouble was that Sue's wedding dress had a spring-steel bustle. When she hit the ground, the bustle bounced her right up again. She went so high her head almost hit the moon. Then she came down again, and bounced again—and she kept right on doing it. She was a bouncing bride, and no mistake.

Sue kept bouncing for nearly a day. It looked as though she never would stop.

High Pockets said to Bill, "Better shoot her, before she starves to death. It would be a kindness, Bill."

Bill wouldn't hear of it. At last he thought of using his big lariat. He lassoed Sue, pulling her down to earth again. Sue looked him straight in the eye, her temper just a-boiling.

"The idea!" she said. "Shamin' me in front of my weddin' guests! Lettin' me git on a hoss I couldn't ride!"

"But I tried to tell you," Bill said.

"Yes, but you didn't stop me! I'm not gittin' hitched with you, Pecos Bill. A man who'd do a thing like that to his bride can't be trusted. Good-by—and if I never see you again, it will be too soon!"

Turning her back on Bill, she walked away. Bill let her go, thinking she'd come back. When she didn't, Bill left his ranch. Working as a cowhand, he searched for Sue in Wyoming and Montana, Arizona and New Mexico, and in Colorado, too. But there wasn't a sign of her. Bill was so brokenhearted that he gave up the cow business and went prospecting for gold.

After staking out a claim, Bill started to dig. He dug deeper and deeper without striking pay-dirt. By the time he stopped digging, he'd dug out the Grand Canyon, which hasn't been filled in to this day.

Feeling a bit thirsty after all that work, Bill dropped in at the Last Chance Hotel.

He said to the bartender, "Give me a glass of lemon pop—straight."

It was Bill's favorite drink, next to carbolic acid. Some bad men who were hanging around looked at Bill. They laughed and called him a tenderfoot.

"Smile when you say that, stranger," said Bill, reaching for his shooting irons.

He was a little out of practice, and the bad men beat him to the draw. Twelve shots rang out, and twelve bullets came at Bill. Thinking fast, Bill lowered his head. When the smoke cleared away, six bad men were stretched out on the floor. The bullets had bounced off Bill's head, hitting the bad men in their shooting arms.

The folks in the town came running, crowding around Bill. They shook his hand and slapped his back. Then and there, they elected him sheriff. Before a week passed, Bill had cleaned up the town. Word about Bill spread, and folks rode in to see him from Tombstone, Dodge City, and a hundred other places. Every town in the West wanted Bill for sheriff, so he could give them law and order.

Bill did the best he could. He went from town to town, cleaning each one up in a day or two. The bad men saw they didn't have a chance, and it got so that Bill didn't even have to go after them. They came to him.

"Throw us in the hoosegow, Bill," they said. "Lock us up. We'll be safer that way."

"Glad to oblige," Bill said.

By and by there wasn't a bad man left. The sheriffs had no trouble at all keeping law and order, and the West really began to grow.

After that, Bill took a sort of vacation. He traveled around the country with a rodeo show. That was his idea, too—he'd thought up the rodeo in his spare time. One day, when he was in California, he invented cowboy movies. He didn't mean to. He was talking to some movie men, telling them stories of the Old West. Bill made up a few whoppers, the way any cowboy would do. The movie men believed them, so Bill made up a few more. The first thing he knew, there were cowboy movies in all the theaters. The movie men had used Bill's whoppers, leaving out the rest.

Bill laughed so hard that some folks say he laughed himself to death, but it wasn't so. Bill went back to the West, and soon he came across a dude ranch. Bill looked at the dudes, dressed up in their fancy Western clothes and trying to act like cowboys.

"Stranger," Bill said to a dude, "are you a human?"

"Why, of course," the dude said.

"And all them other dudes—are they humans, too?"

"Certainly."

"Then I quit!" yelled Bill. "I'm goin' back to bein' a coyote, tail or no tail!"

And he did. Every moonlit night he sits on a hill with the other coyotes, howling at the moon. And sometimes, between howls, he laughs fit to bust.

Anthony and the Mossbunker

From old Amsterdam in the Old World, to New Amsterdam in the New World, came Anthony Van Corlear. He did not cross the great ocean alone, for he was only a boy. With him came his mother and father, his sisters and brothers, and an aunt and an uncle or two. And with him came his shiny brass trumpet.

Now the trumpet was large for a trumpet, and Anthony was small for a boy. So the trumpet was almost as big as Anthony. He did not mind. Every day he polished the trumpet, until it shone like the sun. Every night he took it to bed with him. He did not let it out of his sight for a minute.

When the ship sailed into the harbor at New Amsterdam, Anthony carried his trumpet ashore. Holding it under his arm, he looked around. The first thing he saw was a jolly fat man, who was standing under a tree.

Anthony said to the man, "Mynheer," which is Dutch for mister. "Mynheer," he said, "where is the trumpeter of New Amsterdam?"

The man said to Anthony, "Younker," which is Dutch for youngster. "Younker," said the man, "in New Amsterdam we have almost everything an honest Dutchman could want. We have the good grass and the trees. We have the fields for the cows and pigs, and we have the

23

cows and pigs. We have the broad Hudson River. And in the river we have the fishes, like the sturgeon and the mossbunker. We have the Bowling Green for bowling ninepins. We have the fort to protect us, and we have the fine house for the governor. We have the windmill to grind our grain. And we have the Indians. Ah, yes, the Indians. But a trumpeter? No. A trumpeter in New Amsterdam we do not have."

"Good," said Anthony. "Then I will be the trumpeter of New Amsterdam."

"Indeed!" said the man. "Well, you can start now by playing me a tune."

Anthony hung his head.

He said, "I cannot. I am too small. I cannot breathe in enough air to blow the trumpet."

"Then you will never be the trumpeter of New Amsterdam," said the man. "Why not give me your trumpet? I am round and fat. I can breathe in enough air to blow twenty trumpets."

But Anthony would not give up his trumpet to anyone. He was small, but he, too, could grow round and fat. And so, at breakfast, dinner, and supper, he heaped his plate high. He took double helpings of roast pork or beef or chicken, and pancakes and boiled potatoes as well. Between meals, he ate still more. He ate crullers, doughnuts, honey cake, ginger cake, and Dutch oly koek. He ate pies of every kind, and plum and peach and quince preserves. He drank bowls of milk and heavy cream. And when he was not eating, he practiced breathing in air.

Sometimes, in the summer, he played tag with the boys, or watched the men bowling on the Bowling Green. In the winter he went skating on the frozen ponds, or rode his sled. But mostly he ate, and practiced breathing in air.

In time, from eating so much, his stomach became

round and fat. From breathing in so much air, his nose became large and red and shiny. And, at last, he was able to breathe in enough air to blow his trumpet. He raised it to his lips, blowing a blast that was heard all over town.

The good people of New Amsterdam ran out of their houses.

"What's that?" they said.

Once again they heard the trumpet, loud and clear and sweet.

"Ah!" they said. "Anthony is playing his trumpet. Now he will be the trumpeter of New Amsterdam."

After that, whenever a trumpet was needed, they sent for Anthony. He played at parades and weddings and dances. By this time he was a man, and his whiskers started to grow. But Anthony never shaved. The sharp razor might cut his lip, and he would not be able to play his trumpet any more. He let his whiskers grow longer and longer, while he grew rounder and fatter, and his nose grew larger and redder and shinier.

When Peter Stuyvesant, the new governor, came to town, Anthony was asked to play the trumpet. Peter Stuyvesant was coming by ship from the Old World, just as Anthony had done years ago. People marched down to the harbor to welcome the new governor. Leading them all was Anthony. He wore a fine blue coat with brass buttons, and black shoes with silver buckles. It was hard to tell which shone the most—the buttons, the buckles, the trumpet, or his big red nose.

Anthony cheered with the rest as the ship sailed in. He bowed low when Peter Stuyvesant came down the gangplank. One of the governor's legs had been shot off in the wars. In its place, he wore a wooden pegleg. Now he clomped over the cobblestones until he saw Anthony.

"You, there! Who are you?" Peter Stuyvesant asked.

"I am Anthony, the trumpeter of New Amsterdam."

"And how did you get to be trumpeter?"

"By blowing my own trumpet."

"Let me hear you play," said Peter Stuyvesant.

"Gladly, Mynheer."

Anthony parted his long whiskers with one hand. He raised the trumpet to his lips, took a deep breath, and blew. And as he blew, there was a shout from the crowd. The mighty blast of the trumpet had blown Peter Stuyvesant splash into the bay.

Rushing forward, Anthony helped pull Peter Stuyvesant out of the water. The governor waved his arms, scattering water over everyone. He stamped his wooden leg and roared at Anthony in Dutch.

"Poor Anthony!" wailed the crowd. "The governor has a fierce temper! He will throw Anthony into jail for life! New Amsterdam will be without a trumpeter!"

But before Peter Stuyvesant could order Anthony to be taken away, a man came galloping up on horseback.

"Indians!" he cried. "The Indians are coming!"

"Send them away! I do not wish to see Indians!" bellowed Peter Stuyvesant.

"You do not understand, Governor," said the man on horseback. "We must fight the Indians, or they will capture us. We must get our guns and go into the fort."

All around Anthony the people were shouting and yelling and telling each other what must be done. Anthony said nothing. He just ran. And he did not stop running until he reached the Indians. Climbing up on a rock, once again he raised his trumpet. Once again he took a deep breath, and once again he blew. He blew such a long, loud blast that the Indians nearest him became deaf. As for the rest, the terrible noise stopped them in their tracks. The next minute, every last Indian ran back into the woods.

Oh,.how the good people of New Amsterdam cheered when they heard the news! And Peter Stuyvesant said to Anthony, "You are a brave man, Anthony Van Corlear. You and your trumpet are worth a regiment of soldiers. You shall be my trumpeter, and stand guard against our enemies."

And so Anthony became the governor's trumpeter. On his trumpet he hung the banner of New Amsterdam, with the picture of a beaver on it. From morning to night Anthony stood guard at the fort.

Peter Stuyvesant liked having his trumpeter with him wherever he went. Once he took Anthony along on a trip up the Hudson River. As their ship passed the mountain called the Dunderberg, Anthony was standing at the rail. The sun was high in the sky, and Anthony's nose looked redder and shinier than ever. Suddenly a ray of sunlight bounced off Anthony's nose and hit a huge sturgeon in the water. Hauling in the fish, Anthony found that the sunlight had cooked it nicely.

The fish was served for dinner, and there was enough for all. Peter Stuyvesant said it was the most delicious sturgeon he had ever tasted. And cooked just right, too. He was so pleased he gave a big hill nearby the name of Anthony's Nose.

The people of New Amsterdam were prouder than ever of their trumpeter. Children followed Anthony about on the streets. Men slapped him on the back, and the ladies kissed him. Besides standing guard at the fort, he still played at weddings and dances and parades. And he

would have lived out the rest of his life in happiness, if it had not been for the King of England.

Not that the King had anything against Anthony. To tell the truth, the King had never even heard of him. But many Englishmen had settled in New Amsterdam. The King thought it was silly for the Dutch to own the city when there were so many Englishmen there. So he sent his navy over the sea to take the city away from the Dutch.

As soon as Peter Stuyvesant heard about this, he sent for Anthony.

He said, "Anthony Van Corlear, trumpeter, you must go and warn all our people. Blow your trumpet, so that they will know the English are coming. Every Dutchman must be warned."

"Do not fear, Governor," said Anthony. "They will be warned."

Picking up his trumpet, Anthony went out into the night. He leaped up on his horse, which was as round and fat as he was. And just as he did, thunder roared and the rain began to fall.

Anthony only laughed.

"Ha!" he said. "I will play a duet with the thunder!"

As he rode through the streets, he blew his trumpet, while the thunder boomed like a big bass drum. It was close to midnight when Anthony reached the Harlem River. He jumped off his horse, looking for the ferry that would carry him across. Except for the flashes of lightning, it was so dark he could see no further than the end of his nose. But one thing was certain. There was no ferry on the river that night.

"Well, no matter. You must swim across," he said to his horse.

At these words, the horse reared up on its hind legs. With a fearful neigh, it galloped off. Anthony was left alone on the river bank in the pouring rain, his nose and his trumpet shining out as the lightning flashed.

"The horse is right. This is the very devil of a night," said Anthony. Then, shaking his fist, he roared, "But I will cross the river, *in spite of the devil!*" He spoke in Dutch, and his last words sounded like "Spuyten Duyvil."

Holding his trumpet above his head, Anthony jumped into the water. He had swum about half way across, when a streak of lightning struck beside him. There was a terrible clap of thunder, and out of the water rose a mossbunker. But this was no ordinary mossbunker. It was more than a hundred feet long. It had two extra pairs of eyes, and teeth as sharp as swords. Smoke poured from its gills. And from its mouth came a tongue of flame, and the strong smell of sulphur.

Quickly Anthony put his trumpet to his lips. He blew a great blast, a mighty blast, the mightiest he had ever blown. It was heard for miles around, from the Bowling Green to the Dunderberg.

The mossbunker drew back, blinking its three pairs of eyes. Then its fiery tongue shot out, and its mouth closed on Anthony's leg. Down, down under the water went Anthony and the mossbunker. There was a crash of thunder, the last echo of Anthony's trumpet—and that was all.

Where the mossbunker took Anthony, nobody knew. Neither was ever seen again. With their trumpeter gone, the Dutch soon gave up to the English. But they never forgot Anthony. After that night, no Dutchman would eat a mossbunker, even of ordinary size. The place where Anthony went down they called Spuyten Duyvil.

And sometimes, on a night of wind and rain, Anthony's trumpet can still be heard. Sweet and clear it sounds, from the Bowling Green to the Dunderberg, echoing over the thunder of the storm.

Old Stormalong

MANY a good sailor has sailed the seven seas. But the greatest and biggest of them all was old Stormalong.

Aye, Alfred Bulltop Stormalong was a full-grown man. From his bottommost footbone to his topmost headbone, he measured four fathoms tall. And his size was his trouble, for ships weren't built big enough for him. Most times he couldn't even sleep in the fo'c'sle with the other sailors. He had to curl up on deck.

Come rain, buckets of water poured down on his face. Come frost, he sprouted icicles wherever icicles could sprout. Come fair weather or foul, the skippers complained that his snoring blew the ship off its course. And a man gets tired of that kind of thing.

At last Stormalong shipped out on the *Lady of the Sea,* which was the largest vessel afloat. Large as she was, she still didn't suit his size. And so, coming into port at New Bedford, Stormalong packed his seabag. With some of the crew he went ashore. They made for Billy the Lobsterman's inn, where Stormalong ordered shark soup. As always, he drank it from a dory.

After he'd swallowed the soup, Stormalong said, "Shipmates all, my seafarin' days are over. They don't make ships big enough for me, and a man gets tired. So I'm going to put an oar on my shoulder, and walk to where folks know nothing of the sea. Aye, I walks and I walks, until somebody asks, 'What's that stick on your shoulder?' And there I stops, and there I stays, and there I starts farmin'."

"Not farmin'!" said his shipmates, shaking in their boots.

"Aye, mates, farmin'," said Stormalong.

A man who had been sitting in a corner stood up and came close to Stormalong. He was Captain Starbuck, of the whaling ship *Nancy Ann*.

"Avast there, Stormy!" he said. " 'Tis a fearful thing for a sailor to go farmin'."

"But the ships aren't big enough for me," said Stormalong. "I tell you a man gets tired. I guess I just wasn't meant to sail the sea."

Captain Starbuck said, "Maybe you weren't meant for sailin'. But have you ever been whalin'?"

Stormalong laughed. "Begging your parding, captain," he said, "for I makes small of no man. But I am a deep-water sailor, and not a fisherman what pulls little fishes out of the sea. I'll not go fishin' for whales."

"Why, you lubberly swab!" roared Captain Starbuck. "A whale is no more a fish than I am! A whale is a critter, that's what! And a full-grown critter at that, just right to be hunted by a full-grown man! Come a-whalin' with me, Stormalong, and you'll be the greatest whaler that ever was."

Captain Starbuck was a good talker, and a fast talker. He talked to Stormalong for an hour or more. And in the end Stormalong said, "I'll try it, captain! I'll try it!"

And so Stormalong went a-whaling with Captain Starbuck in the whaler *Nancy Ann*. They sailed to the middle of the ocean, where they dropped anchor. High atop the mast, a lookout in the crow's nest kept an eye out for whale.

Soon he sang out, "Thar she blows! Whale off the port bow! Thar she blows! And thar blows another! And another! And yet another! So help me, mates, it's a whole school of whales! School of whales off the port bow! And thar they blows and breaches!"

"All hands forward! H'ist the anchor!" ordered the captain.

And all hands heaved on the anchor line, Stormalong among them. But the anchor didn't move an inch.

"Heave, you shellbacks, heave!" said Captain Starbuck, and they heaved.

And still the anchor didn't move.

"Blows!" called out the lookout. "Whales off the port bow! Thar they blows! Thar they breaches! Blo-o-o-ows!"

Captain Starbuck jumped up and down, waving his arms.

"Oh, did ever a captain have such a crew!" he yelled.

"Whales off the port bow—a whole school of whales—
and you can't haul up the anchor! Call yourselves
whalers? You're a crew of tailors!"

"Calm yourself, captain—I'll see what's holdin' down
the mudhook," said Stormalong.

He jumped over the side, diving into the ocean. And
where Stormalong dived, the waves reared up. There was
a churning and a roaring under the sea, and the ship
shook from stem to stern. And then the waves were quiet,
and Stormalong climbed aboard again.

"Begging your parding, sir," he said to Captain Starbuck. "But you may order the mudhook to be h'isted."

"Heave!" said Captain Starbuck, and the sailors heaved.
And this time the anchor came up like nothing at all.

"What was it, Stormy?" the captain asked.

"Just an octopus. He was holding on to the anchor with half his arms, and holding on to the sea bottom with the other half. I tied 'em all up into knots. That octopus won't be botherin' us again, sir."

With the anchor hauled up, it didn't take long for the *Nancy Ann* to reach the whales.

"Lower the boats, lads! Lower away!" Captain Starbuck ordered.

The men lowered the whaleboats to the water, ready to row after whales. Picking up a harpoon, Stormalong leaped over the rail. He jumped into a whaleboat, but he was so big he stove a hole right through its bottom. The boat turned over, throwing its crew into the sea.

The other boats stopped chasing whales, and turned back to help. And when the whales saw that, *they* started chasing the boats. Flipping their great tails, they smashed every last boat to bits. Oh, a terrible thing it was, to see all the sailors splashing in the waves, calling for help. By the time they were hauled back aboard the *Nancy Ann*, the whales were gone. And so were the whaleboats. They were all at the bottom of the sea, except for some pieces of planking floating on the water.

"You've done for me, Stormalong!" howled Captain Starbuck. "Whales all about us, and not a boat to give chase! You've done for me, you stretched-out, overgrown, seagoin' elefink! Would that I had never seen the day I asked you to go whalin'!"

"Begging your parding, captain," said Stormalong, "but it couldn't be helped. Those whaleboats are too small for me."

Then he pounded the rail with his fist, and he roared, "I still says whales are fishes, for only fishes lives in the drink! And if they are fishes, I fishes 'em, even though I am a deepwater sailor and not a fisherman what pulls little fishes up out of the sea!"

And he picked up a spare mast, and to the end of the mast he tied a long length of line. To the end of the line he tied a spare anchor. He made him the biggest, longest fishing rod that ever was.

Stormalong got a slab of salt pork from the galley for bait, and hooked it on the anchor. Then, sitting on the jib boom, he cast his line into the water.

Before long, the lookout in the crow's nest sang out, "Thar she blows! Whale off the starboard side! Thar she blows! Thar—thar she bites! And so help me Hannah, thar she's hooked! She's hooked, mates—and a giant of a whale it is!"

Holding the anchor in its mouth, the whale raced across the ocean. It was the biggest whale that ever was in the history of whales, and it pulled the *Nancy Ann* with it.

"Don't lose her, lad!" yelled Captain Starbuck to Stormalong. "She's givin' us a Nantucket sleigh ride!"

Aye, and it was the longest, swiftest, strangest sleigh ride that ever was in the history of whaling. Up and down the ocean went the whale, and behind came the *Nancy Ann*. But the whale was growing weaker, and at last it fetched up near Cape Cod.

Captain Starbuck slapped Stormalong on the back. "You can haul her in now, laddie," he said. "Then we biles the blubber for ile, and we sells the ile, and we'll all be rich. Oh, what a lucky day it was that I asked you to go whalin'! You have invented a new way of catchin' whales, Stormy, and I am the first to say it!"

" 'Tis kindly spoken of you, sir," said Stormalong, starting to haul in the whale.

Just then something rose up in the sea. The lookout shouted, "Sea Sarpint! It's the Cape Cod Sea Sarpint, mates! Thar she goggles! Thar she snorts and splashes! And thar, mercy on us all, thar she bites at the whale!"

"Haul in your whale, Stormalong!" said Captain Star-buck.

But it was too late. The Sea Sarpint splashed in the water, ten fathoms long. Goggling its green eyes, it opened its mouth, showing three decks of teeth. Then it swallowed Stormalong's whale, whole and complete, not forgetting the anchor. It bit through Stormalong's line, coiled up its coils, and sank deep into the sea.

Captain Starbuck had been watching, unable to say so much as a word. Now he threw himself down and kicked his feet against the deck.

"Gone!" he cried. "The biggest whale that ever was! And with it a fortune in ile! Gone and lost forever! And all because of you, Stormalong! You overgrown elefink of a slabsided swab, what fishes for whales with a fishin' rig, instead of catchin' 'em proper! Oh, would I had gone down to Davy Jones' locker, before I saw the day I asked you to go whalin'!"

"Begging your parding, captain," said Stormalong.

"But I have tried sailin', and I have tried whalin'. The ships are too small, and a man gets tired—I am goin' farmin' and you can lay to that."

Jumping over the rail, Stormalong waded in to shore. He put an eighteen-foot oar over his shoulder and turned his back on the sea. He started to walk, and he kept on walking, until a man spoke up to him.

"What's that pole on your shoulder?" asked the man.

At last Stormalong knew that he was far from folks who knew seafaring ways. Sticking his oar into the ground, he said, " 'Twas an oar, mate, but now 'tis just a pole. And here I stops, and here I stays, and here I does me farmin'."

So did Stormalong become a farmer. He farmed early and he farmed late, raising bushels of potatoes, and a few chickens and pigs. And not a word of the sea did he hear or he say, until one morning another farmer stopped by. The farmer leaned against the fence, chewing on a straw and talking.

"Neighbor, you're lookin' thin and peaked," said the farmer. "You sure you like farmin'?"

"I like farmin' fine," said Stormalong. "It couldn't be better. Beats seafarin' all hollow. Nothin' like it. Farmin's just right for a full-grown man."

"Speakin' of seafarin'," said the farmer, "I heard tell of a funny thing. Heard it from my cousin, whose wife's uncle heard it from his brother, who heard it from his son, whose friend knows a fellow that met a man whose sister's husband's grandpa lives in Massachusetts."

"And what did he say?" asked Stormalong.

"That there's a new ship called the *Courser*, which is ten times as big as any ship ever built before."

Stormalong let loose a yell that scared the chickens and worried the pigs and almost knocked the potatoes off the vine.

"Neighbor," he said, "take my farm, and welcome to it. For I have farmed pertaters until I am blue in the face, and a man gets tired. Spuds is fine, mashed with butter, and farmin' is fine for farmers. But I am a deep-water sailor, and if there's a ship big enough for me, I am going back to sea."

And he started down the road, singing:

> Blow, ye winds in the morning,
> And blow, ye winds, high-o
> Clear away your running gear
> And blow, ye winds, high-o!

To New Bedford and to Nantucket, to Marblehead and Cape Cod, went Stormalong, looking for the big ship. But not until he came to Boston did he find the *Courser*. She was so big she couldn't get in the harbor. She was anchored just outside it, sending in her cargo by regular ships.

"Ahoy the *Courser!*" called out Stormalong, jumping into the water. He swam out to the big ship and looked her over fore and aft. She was so big she couldn't be seen in one look, so he looked again. Her masts were so tall they poked through the clouds. The tops were on hinges, and could be put down to let the sun and the moon go by. On deck was a stable of horses, so that the officers could ride to any part of the ship.

"By my boots and breeches!" said Stormalong. "At last I have seen a full-grown ship!"

Singing a gay ditty, he started to climb aboard. As he was pulling himself hand over hand up the anchor chain, the captain and the officers galloped toward him on horse-back. Stormalong's gay ditty turned into a moan, and he almost slid down the anchor chain. For the skipper of the *Courser* was Captain Starbuck, the same who had been on the *Nancy Ann*.

But Captain Starbuck sang out, "It's Stormalong, or I'm a squid! Get on board, lad!"

"You don't bear me a grudge, sir?" asked Stormalong. "After I lost you that whale on the *Nancy Ann?*"

"Why, no," said the captain. "You see, after you lost that whale for me, I had to give up whalin'. I took to plain sailin' again, and in time I got command of this fine ship. If it hadn't been for you, I might still be whalin'. And I would never have been master of the *Courser*, which is the greatest vessel afloat."

He gave Stormalong a squint, and he said, "But what brings you here, lad? I thought you had gone farmin'. And I hates to say it, but you're thin and peaked."

"Aye," said Stormalong. "That comes of lookin' per-taters in the eye the livelong day. Spuds is all right in their place, which is in a dish, mashed, with a bit of salt and plenty of butter. And farmin' is fine for them which is farmers. But I am a deepwater sailor, and I'm askin' if you have a berth for a full-grown man on this full-grown ship."

"I might," said Captain Starbuck. "I just might. I've a crew of six hundred men, and they're good seamen all. But half has to stay aloft, for it takes a week for 'em to climb the rigging. And it takes thirty-six able-bodied men just to turn the wheel and steer."

"Begging your parding, captain, but I could take the wheel alone," said Stormalong.

"Then turn to, Stormy, and take the wheel, for we sail with the tide!" ordered Captain Starbuck.

"Aye, aye, sir!" answered Stormalong. He ran forward to the wheel, with the captain and the officers galloping behind him.

And so did Stormalong go back to sea, on a ship that suited his size. On the *Courser* he slept in the fo'c'sle with the other sailors. Every morning he heard the bosun sing out:

"Rise and shine! Hit the deck, you shellbacks!"

And every morning Stormalong rose, no longer thin and peaked. He did whatever there was to be done, but mostly he took the wheel. The ship gave him very little trouble. She was so big that ordinary storms didn't bother her at all.

But one day, out in the Atlantic, the wind began to howl. It was the start of a storm that was the granddaddy of all storms. There were clouds, and there was fog, and the sky got as black as pitch. Not a thing could be seen, and the sun didn't come out for two weeks. And when it did, Captain Starbuck found that the ship had been blown way off its course. He figured that they were in the North Sea, and headed south, at that.

"It's the end," said Captain Starbuck, mournful as a

fog horn. "The North Sea isn't big enough for us to turn around in! The only way out to the Atlantic Ocean is through the English channel. And we'll never make it, for the *Courser* is too broad to get through! Stormalong, you are a Jonah, what brings bad luck to any ship you board! Oh, would I had gone down to the bottom of the sea before I asked you to come aboard the *Courser!*"

"Begging your parding, sir, but don't give up the ship," said Stormalong.

Climbing up the rigging of the tallest mast, Stormalong looked ahead. Before him he could see the English channel. On one side of it was France, and on the other was England, and the steep cliffs of Dover. With his eye, Stormalong measured the width of the channel. Looking down, he measured the width of the ship likewise. Then he climbed down again and reported to Captain Starbuck.

He said, "The channel is an inch wider than the *Courser*. It will be a tight squeeze, but we can make it."

Carefully Stormalong began to guide the ship through the channel. The officers rode up and down on horseback, watching the sides. As the ship came close to the cliffs of Dover, the third mate called out:

"We're going to bump!"

"Abandon ship! Man the lifeboats!" roared Captain Starbuck. "We'll never make it! And 'tis all your fault, Stormalong, you overgrown swab of a seagoin' elefink of a farmer what calls himself a seaman!"

"Begging your parding, sir," said Stormalong. "But we'll get through yet. Just order all hands to soap the sides so she'll slide through easy-like. Soap her on the starboard side and the larboard, but just a mite more on the starboard."

The captain grumbled, but he ordered all hands to soap the sides. The crew used the finest white soap, rubbing it on the sides until they were slick as glass.

Then Stormalong took the *Courser* through the channel. She squeaked and she creaked, and all the soap on the starboard side scraped off on the cliffs of Dover. But she made it, and the crew raised a great cheer.

"Stormalong," Captain Starbuck said, "I takes back what I said. I most humbly begs your parding. You are not a Jonah what brings bad luck to any ship you board. You are not a swab. You are not a farmer. You are not an overgrown seagoin' elefink, though it's true you're big. You are the greatest deepwater sailor that ever was, and you can lay to that."

So said Captain Starbuck, and so it was. Of all the good sailors that ever sailed the seven seas, the greatest was Stormalong. And yet there are some lubberly swabs who say he never took the *Courser* through the English channel. They say there's no proof. But anyone with half an eye can see that the cliffs of Dover are white. And the reason they're white is that the soap scraped off the side of the *Courser*, and stuck to the rock of the cliffs.

Aye—and if the white cliffs of Dover aren't proof enough for any man, what is?

Johnny Appleseed

Wʜᴇɴ Johnny Appleseed was growing up in Massachusetts, he wasn't Johnny Appleseed. He was called Johnny Chapman, which was his right, true name. But no matter what he was called, his greatest joy was apples.

It wasn't only the taste of them Johnny liked, good as that was. It was the twisty branches of the apple trees in the orchard. It was the apple colors—goldy yellow, and yellowy green, and russet and red. It was the pink and white blossoms at blossom time. Why, even the names of apples started a song in Johnny's head:

Pound Royal, Golden Pippin, Maidenblush, Northern Spy,
For apple sass and cider, fritters and apple pie.
June Red, Roxbury Russet, Fall Wine, Punkin Sweet,
For apple butter and jelly, and to hold in the hand and eat.

Naturally, with such a liking for apples, Johnny had to be an orchardman. He learned to plant the trees, and prune them, and care for them in every way. He lived on his Pa's farm, working in the orchard from sunup to sundown. And there he might have stayed the rest of his born days, except for one thing.

Yes, he could have stayed, and he would have stayed,

except for the road that ran past the farm. Sometimes travelers would come by, afoot or on horseback, or in a wagon. Johnny paid them no mind, being so busy with his apple trees. And then one day a Conestoga wagon loaded with folks stopped before him. The old man who was driving the wagon spoke to Johnny.

"Mornin', young feller," he said. "We'll thank you kindly for a drink of your good well water."

Johnny let them have the water, and some apples besides.

"Where are you going?" he asked.

"We're bound west," the old man said.

"West?" said Johnny. "Where's that? And whatever for?"

"I'll tell you," said the old man, holding up one of Johnny's apples. He laid a long finger on the apple, and he said, "The earth is round, like a big round apple. And we're travelin' west on the big round apple of earth, to make a new home in the wilderness."

"Well, I'll be switched!" said Johnny.

It was a wonder to him, for he was young and had never been away from home. Nor had he thought much about the world, what with all the work there was to do on the orchard. But now that he'd learned he was on the big round apple of earth, he knew what he had to do.

"I reckon I'll go west, too," he said.

In no time at all he told his Ma and Pa goodbye. He was the apple of their eye, and they hated to see him go. But wild horses couldn't hold him back, and away he went in the old man's wagon.

And often, as they journeyed, Johnny asked, "Is this the West?"

And just as often the old man answered, "Not yet, Johnny, not yet."

But when they reached Pittsburgh, the old man nodded his head.

"This is it," he said.

Johnny jumped off the wagon, glad the journey was over. And then he saw that the old man and the folks were going on.

"Where to now, old man?" he asked.

"We're bound west, as I told you," the old man said.

"But this *is* the West."

"There's more," the old man said. "Lots more. We're pushing on down the Ohio Valley to make a home in the wilderness."

"And what might there be in the wilderness?"

"A sight of things," answered the old man. "Trees and rivers and mountains. Wild critters of all sorts, and wild Injuns as well."

"Trees, did you say?" said Johnny. "Apple trees, too?"

The old man shook his head. "There's beech trees, and oak, and maple and pine, and I don't know what all. But nary an apple tree. Oh, some wild crab apple trees, maybe. But not what you'd call a real apple tree. Nary a one."

"I wouldn't like that," said Johnny. "I'll stay here, where there are apple trees a-plenty."

And that's how Johnny came to settle in Pittsburgh. He'd seen a nice spot on a hill for an orchard, and there he made himself a farm. He built a snug house and started to grow apple trees. Besides his orchard, he had bee hives for honey, and chickens for eggs, and cows for milk. He had everything he could want—and yet his mind was troubled.

Because he couldn't help but notice all the folks passing through Pittsburgh, traveling west. There were whole families in wagons, youngsters and oldsters and in-betweens, moving across the big round apple of earth. Johnny thought of them living in the wilderness, with not an apple tree for comfort. He took to giving them apple seeds to raise orchards of their own.

And still Johnny was troubled. Not everybody knew apple trees the way he did. Suppose the trees didn't grow. He hated to think of his good seeds going to waste. And he couldn't forget the folks in the midst of the big, lonely wilderness, far from a helping hand. Johnny worried at it, and around it, and about it—and at last he knew what to do. If he wanted to be sure that apple trees would grow in the wilderness, he would have to see to it himself.

Soon he sold his farm, loaded appleseeds in two canoes, and tied the canoes together. He paddled down the Ohio River, and up the Muskingum, and up White Woman Creek, into the wilderness. And wherever he went, he planted appleseeds. As soon as the seeds were gone, he went back to Pittsburgh for more.

That's when folks began to call him Johnny Appleseed. They laughed at him, too, and they talked.

"He isn't right in his mind," they said. "Else why would he leave a good farm, and go gallivanting all over creation?"

They said, "I hear he wanted to marry a girl, but she wouldn't have him. He's love-cracked."

And they said, "He has a misery that won't let him rest."

Johnny didn't care. He was sure now that his apple trees would grow. They would blossom and bear fruit, and be a comfort to folks for years to come. He packed his seeds in little leather bags and went down into the Ohio valley again. This time he left the canoes behind and tramped along on foot.

Johnny carried no gun or hunting knife. He had his seeds, and a shovel for planting. He had a pot for cooking cornmeal mush, and a Bible to read. When his clothes became ragged, he wore a coffee sack, with holes cut out for his arms and legs. When he lost his cap, he wore his mushpot on his head for a hat. When his shoes wore out, he went barefoot, even in the winter snow.

Into the deeps of the forest he wandered, planting his appleseeds. He walked where the bear walked, and the deer and the fox and the panther. At first he was afraid of the critters, but after a while he wasn't. He never hunted or trapped them, or did them any harm. He liked everything in the woods, down to the smallest of the varmints. If he saw a worm or a ladybug in his path, he'd step aside, to keep from crushing it with his foot.

Once Johnny made a fire to cook his mush. Some mosquitoes came buzzing up, burning themselves in the flame. Johnny poured water on the fire and put it out.

He said, "I'll do without a fire, if it means giving hurt to a living critter."

On a bitter winter night, Johnny crawled into a hollow log to shelter from the cold. He found that a bear and her cubs had got there before him. The bear growled, but Johnny just smiled.

"Now hush," he said. "Rest easy. I'm gettin' out."

And the bear hushed, while Johnny crawled out and went to sleep under a tree.

Another time, Johnny came across a wolf caught in a trap. Johnny turned the wolf loose, and tended to its wounded leg. He might have forgotten all about it, if he hadn't been captured by the Shawnee Indians. They crowded around Johnny, looking at his coffee sack clothes and mushpot hat. They'd never seen anyone like him before. They didn't rightly know what to do with him. One of the old chiefs, who was feeling poorly with a fever, lost his temper. He wanted to scalp Johnny on the spot, and no questions asked.

While the Shawnees were trying to make up their

minds, there was a terrible snarling behind them. They scattered, yelling and carrying on, for that snarling was coming from a wolf. Johnny could tell right off it was the same one he'd saved from the trap.

"No need to run," said Johnny to the Indians, meanwhile petting the critter.

The wolf licked Johnny's hand and sat at his side. The Indians had never seen anything like it. They gave Johnny the run of their camp, sure that he was a medicine man. And Johnny was, in more ways than one. He knew all the forest plants good for sickness. He cured the old chief of his fever and had him up on his feet in a day.

After that, Johnny was a friend of the Indians, and the Indians were friends of his. They even made him a member of the tribe. Johnny stayed with them a while, then wandered on, the wolf trotting at his heels like a dog.

As time went by, folks stopped laughing at Johnny. He was welcome at the cabins of settlers in every corner of the wilderness. If anyone was sick, Johnny would care for him. He always brought some little present for the youngsters—a strange-shaped stone, maybe, or a piece of bright colored cloth for the girls.

It was miles between neighbors, out in the forest, and Johnny carried news from one family to another. He carried another kind of news, too.

"I've got good news from heaven," he'd say to the folks when he came into a cabin. And he would read to them from the Bible he always carried with him.

But Johnny never forgot that his main business was planting apple trees. For forty years he walked the wilderness, moving over the big round apple of earth. The seeds he had planted grew into great spreading trees, heavy with good apples. One day, out Indiana way, he laid himself down under a tree he'd planted so long ago he couldn't remember when.

Johnny was an old man now. His beard was white, and his bones were tired. He watched the blossoms drifting in the soft breeze, falling on him and around him. Slowly his eyes closed, and he seemed to be floating down a long, lazy river. The twisty boughs of apple trees arched overhead, almost hiding the blue sky. Some of the trees were in blossom, and others were bent down with fruit.

Between the trees were fountains of sweet apple cider and wells of apple sass. There were little streams flowing with milk and honey, and bushes that grew apple turnovers and pies. Beside the streams, critters grazed in the green grass, all as friendly as you please. The panther lay next to the deer, and the foxes played with the rabbits. Folks wandered about, eating of the good things around them. The oldsters sat in the warm sun, and the youngsters played at their games in the cool shadows. There were Indians and white folks and folks of all colors, mingling and laughing and having a time.

"It's a dream," said Johnny, "though it needn't be."

And Johnny knew that he would walk the big round apple of earth no more. He smiled, for he had done his work and it was good, and now he could take his rest. And as he dreamed his last dream, and breathed his last breath, he seemed to hear a song from somewhere far away:

Pound Royal, Golden Pippin, Maidenblush, Northern Spy,

For apple sass and cider, fritters and apple pie.

June Red, Roxbury Russet, Fall Wine, Punkin Sweet,

For apple butter and jelly, and to hold in the hand and eat.

Davy Crockett, the Yaller Blossom o' the Forest

Down on the Nola-Chucky River, in the backwoods of Tennessee—that's where Davy Crockett was born. And not long after he was, he wanted to go hunting. He jumped up from his cradle, flapped his arms, and crowed like a rooster.

"I'm the yaller blossom o' the forest!" he said. "I'm half horse, half alligator, and a mite touched with snappin' turtle! I can lick my weight in wildcats! I'm a ring-tailed roarer! The woods is full o' critters to be hunted, and I'm rarin' to go!

"Maybe so, and maybe not," said Davy's Pa.

"Whichever, you're too young for huntin'," said Davy's Ma.

Davy roared riproariously and howled howliferously. The noise almost raised the roof of the cabin. But all that carrying on didn't do him a bit of good. He had to get back in his cradle, which was made of the shell of a snapping turtle three hundred years old.

Little Davy was as foxy as they come. One way or another, he was bound to do some hunting. He waited until his Ma and Pa weren't looking, and made himself a slingshot. He took a handful of dried beans for shot, and stood up in his cradle.

Whirling the slingshot around his head, he popped beans at skeeters, bluebottle flies, and such-like varmints. Davy was a sure shot from the start. He could shoot a fly right off his Pa's nose from across the room. No varmint could last long in the cabin with Davy around.

Soon as he was knee-high to a grasshopper, Davy took to the woods. Right off, he learned everything about the critters and the greenery of the forest. Davy's Ma didn't like him going off in the woods so much. Every time she wanted him, he'd be traipsing around, nobody knew where. There were chores to be done, and it was up to Davy to do them.

Davy saw that his Ma was right. Still and all, it didn't suit him to be in the cabin, when he could be out in the woods. So off he went once more, to where the forest was thickest. And there he found himself a most ferocious panther.

"Whoo-oop!" said Davy to the panther. "I'm Davy Crockett, the yaller blossom o' the forest!"

The panther didn't say a word.

"I'm a ring-tailed roarer, and this is my day to roar!" said Davy.

The panther didn't blink an eye.

"I can fight harder, shoot farther, run faster, jump higher, squat lower, dive deeper and come up drier than any man in these parts!" said Davy.

The panther showed its teeth, growling like small thunder. Davy growled back. The panther sprang at Davy—and Davy sprang at the panther. They were sure to meet, and they did. They tangled and they tussled. They howled and they yowled. Other critters came crowding around to see the fun. All they could see, though, was a big cloud of dust and dirt, of twigs and leaves and rocks flying around. But after a while the cloud died down—and there stood Davy, holding the panther by the tail. The critters jumped up and down, and gave a rousing cheer.

Davy walked home with the panther slung over his shoulder.

"Now don't that beat all!" said his Ma and Pa.

"Oh, it wasn't such a much," said Davy. "You see, I got me a rule—*Be sure you're right, then GO AHEAD!* I knew I was right to battle the panther, so I went ahead. That's all there was to it."

Davy trained the panther to bring in the firewood, and to light the fire with the sparks of its own eyes. It washed the dishes, too, meanwhile sweeping the floor with a broom tied to its tail. Davy's Ma had to admit that a panther was a mighty handy thing to have around the house.

With the panther doing all the chores, Davy had plenty of time to roam the woods. He had time for

frolics and dances, too. It was a real treat to see him step,
while his Pa fiddled and sang out:

> *Ol' Dan Tucker was a good ol' man,*
> *Washed his face in a fryin' pan,*
> *Combed his hair with a wagon wheel,*
> *And died with a toothache in his heel.*

By and by, Davy got older, as boys will. He said to
his Pa, "I'm not as young as I was, or as old as I'll be.
It's about time I started huntin' proper."

"You sure?" said Davy's Pa.

"Well, you know my rule," answered Davy—*"Be sure
you're right, then GO AHEAD!"*

"Are you sure you're right?" asked Davy's Pa.

"Sure for sartin," Davy said.

"Then GO AHEAD!" said Davy's Pa.

He gave Davy a flintlock rifle, named old Betsy, and a
powderhorn for powder. He gave him his pick of the
hunting dogs. Davy picked the ones called Whirlwind,
Old Growler, Old Rattler, Holdfast, and Thunderbolt.

Davy put on a new coonskin cap, moccasins, and a
fringed buckskin shirt and leggings. Then he jumped up
in the air, kicked his heels together, and neighed like
a horse.

"Whoo-oop!" he said. "I'm the yaller blossom o' the
forest! I'm half horse, half alligator, and a mite touched
with snappin' turtle! I can lick my weight in wildcats,
hug a b'ar too close for comfort, and wade the Mississippi!
I'm a ring-tailed roarer, and this is my day to roar!
Whoo-oop!"

And so Davy started off, to go hunting proper. He
hunted the big bear and the little raccoon, and everything in between. He hunted the buffalo and the wildcat,
the panther and the fox, the wolf, the deer, and the
wild boar.

Walking through the woods one day, Davy saw a coon up a tree. Quick as a wink, he raised old Betsy, his flintlock rifle. But before he could pull the trigger, the coon called out:

"Don't shoot, Davy! I'll come down!"

It tickled Davy to know that the critter had heard of him.

"Come along with me," he said. "I won't shoot. Why, I wouldn't hurt a hair o' your head!"

"I believe you, Davy," said the coon. "And I thank you. But just supposin' you was to change your mind!" And away the coon ran, skedaddling through the woods.

After that Davy didn't bother to shoot at coons. He just grinned at them, until they tumbled right down. Once Davy made a mistake. He grinned at a knot on a tree, thinking it was a coon. He grinned such an almighty powerful grin that it burned off all the tree's bark.

Davy hunted in Tennessee and Kentucky, then went on to Arkansas. It was night when Davy got to Whang-doodle Knob. Feeling plumb tuckered out and sleepy, Davy put down old Betsy, his flintlock rifle. He hung his powderhorn on a little yellow twig sticking out in the sky. In the morning Davy looked for his powderhorn, but it was gone. And there wasn't any yellow twig in sight.

"Well, burn my boots," said Davy, "if I didn't hang my powderhorn on a little yaller moon, thinkin' it was a twig! It just goes to show what a body will do when he's sleepy."

Davy had to laugh, but all the same he didn't like it. He would have to wait until the moon came around again before he could get his powderhorn. And without his powderhorn, he couldn't go hunting.

It turned out that Davy wasn't the only one who knew that. A big bear had been watching from behind a rock. He crept up on Davy, giving Davy a most fearsome bear-hug. It would have been the end of anybody else. But Davy wasn't anybody else. He was Davy Crockett, and no bear could get the best of him. He threw *his* arms around the bear, giving that bear the most teetotally fearsome bear-hug that was ever hugged.

"I've a good mind to squeeze you into b'ar jelly, cork it up in your hide, and tote you home," said Davy.

But the bear moaned so, Davy didn't have the heart to do it. He let the bear go and made a pet of him, naming him Death Hug. That bear never forgot Davy's kindness. Once he saved Davy from some Indians. Telling Davy to get on his back, he jumped into a tree. He leaped from one tree to another, carrying Davy until the Indians were out of sight.

Davy liked Death Hug's company so much, he got himself a couple of other pets. One was Mississip, a buffalo. The other was Long Mississip, an alligator. Mississip had a fine bass voice. Around the campfire at night, he and Davy would sing *Hail Columbia* as nice as you please. Death Hug would wave his arms, while Long Mississip beat time with his tail.

Davy figured he'd take his pets home and introduce them to his folks. He made a canoe out of a hollow log and started down the Mississippi River. Davy, Death Hug, and Mississip paddled, and Long Mississip used his tail to steer. Going around a narrow bend in the river, they bumped into something going the other way. It was a log with three kegs fastened to it, one on top of another. In the top keg was a little fat man dressed like a sailor. He wore sailcloth trousers, a leather patch over one eye, and had a little pigtail sticking out from under his hat.

Davy couldn't help but laugh, and the little fat man looked Davy up and down.

"Shiver me mizzen!" he said. "I thought you was a catfish! Out o' me way, ol' rusty bottom, before I turn myself loose!"

His voice was so rough it couldn't be shown in writing.

It would have to be shown in a picture. Davy didn't mind the voice, but he didn't like what the little fat man was saying with it.

"Start travelin'!" said Davy. "Travel far, and travel fast! For I'm Davy Crockett, the yaller blossom o' the forest! I'm half horse, half alligator, and a mite touched with snappin' turtle! Now look out, for I'm goin' through like a flash o' lightnin' through a gooseberry bush!"

"Why, you slabsided landlubber!" said the little fat man. "I'm Ben Hardin, and I'm a snorter and a screamer! Out o' my way, before I turn you inside out! Just step ashore, Davy, and I'll wrestle you fair and square, catch as catch can, no holds barred, and may the best man win!"

"Ben Hardin," said Davy, "better close your mouth before you get your teeth sunburned! I've had enough o' your jawin'! Let's fight!"

They both hopped to shore and started right in wrestling. The way it turned out, they enjoyed it so much they forgot what they were fighting about. So they shook hands, becoming fast friends for life.

While they were talking, black clouds filled the sky. The wind roared and shrieked, bending the trees till they touched the ground. The rain came down, and the river rose up in waves. Thunder thundered thunderiferously, while lightning streaked all about.

Ben Hardin shook and shivered, and quaked and quivered.

He said, "Davy, I'm a man what's seen things. I've seen more with my one eye than most men do with two. I've seen storms at sea and storms on land. I've seen wind storms and rain storms, snow storms and dust storms. I've seen hurricanes galore. But boil me for a sea hoss if I ever saw a storm like this before!"

"It's just a little ol' Mississippi shower," said Davy. "Won't do a bit o' harm. But if you want to move on, nothin' beats lightnin' for fast travel. Just follow me!"

Davy reached out and took hold of a streak of lightning. He jumped on the streak, sitting on it as though it were a horse. Ben jumped on behind, and away they went. Up in the sky, Davy brought out a little bottle of rattlesnake oil. He greased the lightning with it, and they went even faster. It was the first time in history anybody had ever gone as fast as greased lightning.

Davy and Ben stayed on the lightning until it struck in Tennessee. They landed near the cabin of Davy's Ma and Pa, where some folks were waiting to see Davy. Trouble was on its way, and they wanted Davy's help.

"What kind o' trouble?" asked Davy.

The folks answered, "There's a comet comin' through the sky, headin' right for the earth. If it hits us, we're done for."

"Just what kind o' critter is a comet?" asked Davy.

And the folks told him, "It's somethin' like a shootin' star, only ten times as big and twice as sassy. It's a big blazin' ball o' fire, has a long tail, and shoots off sparks."

"Shucks!" said Davy. "Is that all? I'll catch that little ol' comet and wring off its tail."

"No, no, Davy!" said the folks. "That won't do. There's no tellin' what might happen. That comet might explode and blow us all to bits. Or it might put the world on fire. And then where would we be?"

"I don't *have* to wring off its tail. I could shoot 'er full o' holes with ol' Betsy," Davy said.

"That's just as bad. Better think o' somethin' else," said the folks.

"Well, there's more than one way to skin a cat," said Davy. "Suppose you leave it to me. And while you're leavin' it to me, we'll have a frolic. Pa will play his fiddle, and there'll be dancin' by one and all."

The folks couldn't figure what Davy wanted with a

frolic. This was no time to be dancing, with the comet headed for the earth. Davy's Pa couldn't figure it, either.

He said, "You sure you want a frolic, Davy?"

Davy said, "You know my rule, Pa—*Be sure you're right, then GO AHEAD!*"

"You sure you're right?" asked Ben Hardin.

"Sure for sartin," said Davy.

"Then GO AHEAD!" said Davy's Pa.

And he began fiddling on his hemlock fiddle. He was the best fiddler in that neck of the woods, and the folks couldn't help dancing to his music. Soon they were all stepping out, while Davy's Pa fiddled away and called out the calls:

> *Up and down and around and around!*
> *Allemande left and allemande aye!*
> *Ingo bingo, six penny high!*
> *Big pig, little pig,*
> *Root hog or die!*

It wasn't long before Mississip, Long Mississip, and Death Hug came running up. They joined in the dance, shaking a leg right next to Davy and Ben. Everyone went

on dancing till sundown, then kept dancing in the light
of the moon. All of a sudden Ben Hardin looked up and
let out a yell.

"It's the comet!" he said. "Look out! Here it comes!"

And sure enough, there was the comet blazing across
the sky. Straight toward the earth it came, swishing its
tail and shooting out sparks. Ben Hardin and the folks
jumped into the bushes, but Davy kept right on dancing.

"Keep a-fiddlin', Pa!" said Davy. "Fiddle as you've
never fiddled before!"

As the comet came closer, Davy sang:

Turkey in the straw, turkey in the hay,
Roll 'em up and twist 'em up a high tuckahaw,
And hit 'em up a tune called Turkey in the Straw.

And Davy's Pa hit up the tune, fiddling as he'd never
fiddled before. The comet rushed toward the earth—and
then it slowed down. Waggling its tail, it began to bob
and hop in time to the music. Davy bowed to the comet,
and the comet bowed back. And the next thing that
happened, the comet was dancing with Davy. Away they
went, with Davy stomping so hard it sounded like a

surefire earthquake. The folks clapped hands, while Davy's Pa called:

> *Swing that Indian, swing that squaw,*
> *And swing that boy from Arkansaw!*
> *Swing your ma, and swing your pa,*
> *And don't forget your mother-in-law!*

All night long Davy's Pa made music. He fiddled *Old Zip Coon, Fire on the Mountain, Weevily Wheat,* and then some. All night long Davy and the comet danced. They danced the Virginia reel, the double-shuffle, the grind-the-bottle, the buck-and-wing, and lots more. And just before the first light of morning, the comet began to wobble. Davy was still going strong, but the comet had had enough.

Davy leaped up in the air and kicked his heels together.

"Whoo-oop!" he said. "I'm the yaller blossom o' the forest! I can out-dance any critter on land or sea or in the sky! Now let's get on with this frolic, for I'm just gettin' warmed up and I'm rarin' to go!"

But the comet just shook its head. Off it went, leaving the earth and rolling across the sky. It was the most discombobulated comet anyone had ever seen.

"Three cheers for Davy Crockett!" said Ben Hardin. "He's danced the comet down!"

The folks thought so much of Davy for saving them from the comet that they elected him to Congress. Davy made speeches and passed laws, just like any congress-man. The first chance he got, though, he went back to hunting.

And soon after he did, he woke early one morning. The sky was dark, with no sun in sight. The wind howled like a flock of wildcats, and the forest trees were frozen too stiff to shake. Davy had never seen it so cold. He tried to start a fire, but in a minute it had frozen stiff like the trees.

"Looks as if the very daybreak has froze fast," said Davy. "It's up to me to unfriz it, or human creation is done for!"

Davy started up Daybreak Hill, going at a hop, skip,

and jump to keep warm. He stopped just long enough to shoot a bear. Carrying the bear on his back, he walked to the very peak of Daybreak Hill. And now Davy could see all the wheels and gears that made the earth and the sun go around. He could see what the trouble was, too. The earth had frozen fast on its own axis. On top of that, the sun had got jammed between two cakes of ice under the wheels. It had been shining and working to get loose until it froze fast in its own sweat.

Davy squeezed the bear, pouring hot bear oil over the earth and the sun. After they had thawed, he gave the earth's cogwheel a kick to get it loose. In about fifteen seconds the earth gave a grunt and began moving. So did the sun, while the wheels and cogwheels began to turn. As the sun rose up, Davy warmed his hands by the blaze of the sun's top-knot. He put a piece of sunrise in his pocket and walked down the hill again. In no time at all the sun was shining in the sky, and fresh daylight was everywhere.

After that, Davy hunted some, then went off to Texas. Some folks say he was killed fighting at the Alamo. But other folks say it wasn't so. They say Davy is still roaming the woods, with Death Hug, Mississip, and Long Mississip. And whenever you see him, Davy leaps up in the air, kicks his heels together, and neighs like a horse.

"Whoo-oop!" roars Davy. "I'm Davy Crockett, the yaller blossom o' the forest! I'm half horse, half alligator, and a mite touched with snappin' turtle! I can lick my weight in wildcats, wade the Mississippi, and hold a b'ar too close for comfort! I can fight harder, shoot straighter, run faster, jump higher, squat lower, dive deeper, stay under longer, and come up drier than any man in these parts! I'm a ring-tailed roarer, and this is my day to roar! Whoo-oop!"

At least, that's what some folks say.

Sam Patch's Last Leap

SAM PATCH was the pride of the nation, and the joy of one and all. Never was there such a champion jumper, leaper, and diver as this same Sam Patch. He jumped from the roofs of buildings. He jumped from high bridges into deep rivers. He even jumped from mighty Niagara Falls and lived to tell the tale.

Sam made most of his jumps in New Jersey and New York State, but he was a New England Yankee, born and bred. His home was Pawtucket, on the Pawtucket River in Rhode Island. Sam was a baby of about six months when he started his jumping. He leaped from his Grandma's arms right into a washtub full of suds.

"Don't you do that again, Sam Patch!" said his Grandma. "No harm done this time, but that was a mistake, and don't you forget it."

But there was no mistake in Sam Patch. He'd meant to jump. He liked to jump. And jump he did, whenever he got the chance. Once he jumped from the roof of his Ma's henhouse. He was three years old, and there was still a thing or two about jumping he didn't know. He landed smack on a goose—which was fine for Sam, but a little hard on the goose.

"Ma!" said Sam. "Looks like we'll be having roast goose for supper!"

As Sam grew older, he kept on jumping. He was a wonder at leapfrog. In school he was smart enough, but a little slow at reading. He couldn't help jumping over the big words. A likely lad he was, though jumpy.

And then at last Sam was old enough to go out and earn his keep.

"Son," said his Pa, as pas did in Pawtucket, "it's time you chose your callin'. Choose it well and choose it careful, for I'd like to see you rise in the world."

"No better way to rise than by jumping," said Sam.

Sam's Pa frowned. "No, that won't do. You may rise, but you're bound to fall. How about being a lawyer?"

"I haven't the head for it, Pa," answered Sam.

"Well," said Sam's Pa, "honest labor is no disgrace. Many a man has risen high from a lowly start. Would you care to be a blacksmith?"

"I haven't the back for it," said Sam.

"A carpenter?"

"I haven't the hand for it."

"A watchmaker, maybe?"

"I haven't the eye for it."

"How about a music teacher?"

"No, Pa. I haven't the ear for it."

"Then you must go into the cotton mill and be a cotton spinner, just like me."

"I haven't the heart for it," said Sam.

"Heart or not," said Sam's Pa, "you must do something. There are jobs to be had at Slater's mill, and there'll be a place for you."

"Yes, Pa," said Sam, and he started to work as a cotton spinner. It looked as though his jumping days were over.

But Slater's mill was on the bank of the Pawtucket River. After work on hot days, the mill boys would climb the roof and jump into the water. Sam did the same, and of course he was the best jumper of all, climbing higher and leaping farther. He was making a name for himself as a jumper in Pawtucket, when things slowed down at Slater's. Sam's Pa moved his family to Paterson, New Jersey, where Sam went to work at another mill.

Sam was a fair cotton spinner. He wasn't too good, but he wasn't too bad. All the same, he wasn't rising any in the world, and his Pa was worried. Along about that time Captain Enoch Wentworth, an old seagoing friend of Pa's, dropped in between voyages. The captain listened while Pa told all about Sam.

"No need to worry about the lad," said Captain Enoch. "Send him to sea. I'll make a seaman out of him, and there's no better callin'."

And so Sam went off with Captain Enoch to try his luck as a sailor. The captain's ship was anchored at Hoboken, and Sam and the captain had to get to it in a rowboat. On the way a wind blew up, and the boat tossed and rolled a bit. It was nothing to speak of, and even less than that to an old seaman like Captain Enoch. But Sam Patch turned green in the face and dizzy in the head. He hung over the side, like the landlubber he was.

When they reached the ship, Sam said, "Send me back, captain. I'll never make a sailor. I haven't the stomach for it."

"Blast me for an old swab if I ever see the like!" roared Captain Enoch. "You've no head for lawin', no back for smithin', no hand for sawin', no eye for watchmakin', no ear for music teachin', no heart for cotton spinnin'— and now you tell me you've no stomach for the sea! Man, what's left of you? And what's to become of what's left? I promised your Pa I'd make a seaman of you, and I never go back on a promise. Now get on board and fall to, before you feel the toe of me boot!"

Sam sadly got on board, and then his eye fell on the tall mainmast. And a gleam came into that eye as he looked at the mast, and he said, "Captain, I'm a jumper by trade—and this is as good a place to jump as any."

Before he could be stopped, Sam was climbing up the mast. On the deck below, Captain Enoch was bellowing, "Belay there! There'll be no skylarkin' and lallygaggin' on my ship! For the bottom of the sea is made for fishes, and the top of the sea is made for honest sailin' by honest sailormen, and I'll have no leapin' and jumpin' betwixt the two!"

By this time Sam was standing on the topmost tip of the mast, balancing on his toes.

"Behold!" he sang out. "The Jersey Jumper will try a small leap, just to show that some things can be done as well as others."

People came crowding to the edge of shore, and to the decks of ships all about, to see what was going on.

"Better get down!" someone called out. "It will be a mistake to jump!"

"There is no mistake in Sam Patch," answered Sam.

And he leaped into the air, and away he went, feet first and toes down, into the water. He swam to the ship, climbed aboard, and bowed to the crowd.

"Well, Captain Enoch," he said. "I guess that shows that some things can be done as well as others."

"Aye," Captain Enoch said. "Jumpin's your callin', right enough, Sam Patch. But I never heard tell of anyone earnin' his keep by such outlandish stunts."

Just then coins came clinking and chinking on deck, tossed there by the cheering crowd. It was more gold and silver than Captain Enoch had ever seen at one time—or Sam, for that matter.

Sam smiled and waved to the crowd.

"That shows you again, captain," he said. "Daring deeds bring their own reward. I'll get along. It will keep me jumping, but I don't mind."

Wishing the captain a pleasant farewell, Sam left the ship. He journeyed to Passaic Falls, where a crowd had gathered to watch a new bridge be pulled across the water. It was Sam's chance to jump, and he jumped at the chance. He climbed a tall pine tree on the edge of the high cliff over the river. He made a little speech and then jumped, feet first, toes together, the way he always did. A great cheer came from the crowd as Sam hit the water, and another as he swam back to shore. Nobody cared about the bridge—it was Sam all the way.

After that, Sam made jumps from bridges all over New Jersey and New York. Everywhere people thronged to see him. They said Sam was the greatest jumper ever seen in this or any other country.

And yet Sam was not satisfied. The bridges he jumped from were high, but he wanted to rise even higher in the world. He wanted to try something new and different that had never been jumped before. Sam gave it some thought—and then he had it. Niagara Falls! Never had anyone leaped into Niagara's roaring waters and come out alive. But Sam Patch could do it, and Sam Patch *would* do it, to show that some things can be done as well as others.

The day Sam was to jump the Niagara, crowds of people came to the falls. Men, women and children stood on the American side, and on the Canadian side as well. They looked at the scaffolding Sam had built on Goat Island, and the platform high on its top, with the American flag flying over all.

"Here he comes! Here's Sam Patch!" they cried, when Sam walked out among them. He wore blue pantaloons and coat, a white shirt, and a big red handkerchief around his neck.

Some of the people tried to hold Sam back. "Don't jump!" they said. "You're a brave man, Sam Patch, but nobody can jump the falls! It's goodbye to you forever if you do!"

Sam only smiled and waved, as cool as you please. He took off his shoes and he took off his coat. Slowly he climbed up the ladder to the platform. It swayed as he stood on it. He pulled off his red handkerchief, tied it around his waist, and kissed the American flag that fluttered from the scaffold. Rain began to fall, splashing around him. Below him crashed the falls. There was water, water, everywhere, with Sam in the midst.

"He can't do it! He won't jump!" came voices from the crowd. "And if he does, he won't make it! Don't jump, Sam! It'll be a mistake!"

Sam smiled and raised his arms. He leaped into the air. Feet first, toes down, he fell like an arrow. He hit the roaring, rushing water, and his head went under.

"He is lost!" shrieked the crowd. "He's dead! Oh, poor Sam Patch! What a mistake!"

In a minute Sam's head bobbed up, followed by the rest of him, as he scrambled to shore.

"There is no mistake in Sam Patch," he said.

The crowd let out a sigh, then gave him many a "Hurrah!" and "Huzza!" Men, women and children laughed and cried. They waved handkerchiefs and threw hats in the air. "This is the real Sam Patch," they said. "There's never been a jumper like him in the history of the world!"

Sam's great feat made his name known far and wide. Everywhere folks talked of Sam Patch, and tried to jump like Sam Patch. Boys jumped from trees and barns. Clerks jumped over their counters. Farmers jumped over their fences. Sailors jumped ship. But of course no one could jump like Sam Patch.

The hero of all the nation was Sam. He had risen high in the world. He had fame and fortune. He had fine clothes and money to jingle in his pocket. He even bought himself a pet bear, which he led around on a golden chain. It would have been enough, and more than enough, for most men. But not for Sam Patch. As long as there

were places left to jump, he would jump them. But where could he find a more daring jump than Niagara Falls?

And then one day, as Sam was going out walking with his pet bear, three gentlemen came up to him.

Bowing and raising their hats, they said, "Do we have the honor, sir, to address Sam Patch?"

"You do, gentlemen," said Sam. "This is the real Sam Patch, and no mistake."

"Our respects, sir," said the three gentlemen. "We come from the city of Rochester, and we wish to invite you to jump the Genesee Falls."

"I know of your fair city," said Sam, "and I know of your falls. What you say interests me greatly."

The three gentlemen nodded. "We wish to be fair, sir. It is only right to tell you that the Genesee Falls is a dangerous falls. Perhaps, in some ways, it is more dangerous than Niagara. No one has ever dared to jump it."

Sam Patch folded his arms on his chest and held his head high.

He said, "Sam Patch dares. And what Sam Patch dares, Sam Patch does. Gentlemen, you have your answer."

The next day posters were pasted up everywhere, saying:

HIGHER YET!

SAM'S LAST JUMP!

SOME THINGS CAN

BE DONE AS WELL

AS OTHERS!

THERE IS NO MISTAKE

IN SAM PATCH!

All up and down the Genesee valley went the word, and people rushed to Rochester. They came by wagon and coach, by schooner and horse, and even by foot. They

jammed the banks of the Genesee River, and the roofs
and windows of every building around.

There was much arguing among them, and even a fist
fight or two. Many were sure Sam couldn't jump the
Genesee, and many just as sure he could. But one and all
joined in a rousing cheer when Sam stepped out on the
rock that overhung the falls. He was leading his pet
bear, which he tied to a tree. He took his red handkerchief from his neck and tied it around his waist. He
climbed up the scaffold on the rock, stood on the platform, and raised his hands for silence.

"Ladies and gentlemen," he said, and his voice could
be heard above the roar of the water. "Great deeds have
been done in the world by great men. One such was
Napoleon, who conquered nation after nation. He, in
turn, was conquered by Wellington, who so became
greater than Napoleon. But with all their greatness,
could either of them jump the Genesee?"

"No!" came the answer from the crowd.

"A thousand times no!" said Sam. "They left that to your humble servant, Sam Patch. And now, before your very eyes, at this very moment, ladies and gentlemen, Sam Patch does what Napoleon and Wellington could not!"

"Look before you leap, Sam!" someone called out.

But Sam did not look. He leaped. Through the air and under the water he went—and under the water he stayed. He sank into the river like a stone and never came up again. Strong men sobbed, and the tears of the ladies flowed like the waters of the Genesee itself. The river was searched, but no trace of Sam could be found. Ah, a sad, sad day it was for Rochester and the nation.

Now there were many in the crowd who knew that Sam liked nothing better than a good joke. They said that Sam was just playing a trick. Maybe he hadn't jumped at all, but had pushed a dummy into the river. Or, more likely, he had swum behind a rock, and was hiding there this minute. He'd surely turn up the next day, enjoying a good laugh at one and all.

Later, some folks said he *did* turn up. One man told of seeing Sam in the streets of Albany, as large as life. Another told of seeing him in Canandaigua, bound for New Jersey. Still another told of seeing him in the twilight at Genesee Falls, jumping for a crowd of fishes. Be that as it may, the only man who really found out what happened to Sam was Captain Enoch Wentworth. And not a word of it did the captain whisper to anyone. He had his reasons, too, old Captain Enoch had.

It happened that not long after Sam made his last leap, Captain Enoch was whaling in the South Seas. While cruising about, he put in at an island, to take on some fresh water. No sooner had he set foot on shore, than he stopped. For he had seen many a marvel in his day, but never anything like what he saw now. And what he saw was a man under a palm tree, dressed in blue pantaloons, with a white shirt, and a red handkerchief around his neck.

"You, there!" said Captain Enoch, pointing a long finger. "You there, under the palm tree, a-eaten' of mangoes and pangoes and such-like fruit! Be you Sam Patch, or be you a ghost?"

"It's the real Sam Patch, and no mistake," said Sam. "Hello, captain!"

"Why, Sam, I thought you were drowned in the Genesee," said Captain Enoch. "How *on earth* did you get here?"

"I didn't get *on* earth here at all," Sam answered. "I came right slap *through* it! After leaping from the falls, I went so everlasting deep, I thought it was just as short to come up on the other side, so out I came in these parts. I liked it here, so here I stayed, and here I am."

Captain Enoch still wasn't sure that this was the real Sam Patch. But he had a nice visit, filled his water casks, and returned to his ship. As it set sail, Sam climbed a palm tree. He jumped into the air, leaping over the ship's tallest mast, and landed on an island on the other side.

"Farewell, Captain Enoch!" said Sam, leaping from island to island, over that blue South Seas sea.

And Captain Enoch knew then that this was the real Sam Patch. But who would believe it if he said that Sam had jumped through the earth and come out in the South Seas? Besides, it was none of his business. Sam could speak for himself when he got back to New Jersey. And so not a word did Captain Enoch say, only smiling when he heard talk of Sam being seen here or there.

As for Sam himself, he never did go back to Jersey. He stayed in the South Seas. And, for all anyone knows, he's there yet, leaping from island to island over that blue South Seas sea.

Paul Bunyan

Talking about Paul Bunyan, let's get one thing straight. Paul was a big man. How big? Well, he always used a pine tree to comb his beard. It wasn't a full grown pine tree, of course. But it wasn't just a little old sapling, either.

Paul's blue ox, Babe, was pretty sizeable, too. Babe weighed fourteen tons and three ounces, including his bright blue color. He measured exactly twenty-seven ax handles and a plug of Star tobacco from eye to eye. Paul could keep Babe in line without any trouble—which gives you a rough idea of Paul's size.

Some folks say Paul was born in the state of Maine, some say in Canada. Whichever, he wasn't any different from most babies. It's true he had a long, curly beard and weighed eighty-six pounds. But that wasn't surprising. All the men in Paul's family had long beards, and every one of them weighed twice as much.

Paul waited until he learned to walk before he made up his mind to be a logger. Then he took to hanging around the lumberjacks at a logging camp near his home. At first the loggers wouldn't let him do a real job of work. Paul was eight feet tall and had a beard, but he still talked baby-talk. Anybody could see he wasn't a grown-up man.

"Looky here, son," said the loggers, handing him an ax. "You're too young for loggin'. We'll make you our chief day-breaker."

It was only meant for a joke, of course. But the next morning, Paul was up before the sun. He ran up a mountain, and two hours before the sun was due to rise, broke day with his ax. Rushing back to camp, he woke the loggers with a holler so loud it blew the blankets out the window. The loggers shivered with the cold and lost two hours of sleep. The laugh was on them, all right.

As Paul grew up, he became bigger and better and stronger and smarter. Outside of that, he didn't change much. But the United States changed a lot. Up to that time, the country was almost as flat as a pancake. It hardly had any geography to it at all. There were just a few little mountains and rivers and such scattered around. It was pretty, but kind of tiresome.

Changing the country was all Paul's doing. He made more geography than any ten other men, and here's how. Soon as he knew everything there was to know about logging, he lit out to set up a camp of his own. He hired Hals Halvorsen for his foreman, and Johnny Inkslinger for his bookkeeper. He hired Sourdough Sam and Hot Biscuit Slim for his cooks. And he hired hundreds of men for ordinary loggers.

Paul figured on getting started somewhere in the North Woods, around Michigan or Minnesota. He aimed to build the biggest logging camp that ever was, and everything had to be just right. He saw that a camp like that would need plenty of water. So he dug the Great Lakes to hold his water supply. He hauled the water to his camp in a big tank, pulled along by Babe.

One day the tank sprung a leak, and the water came busting out. It looked as though the whole United States would be flooded and washed into the sea. But Paul was a fast thinker. Grabbing a shovel, he dug a long ditch to drain off the water. Later this ditch was known as the Mississippi River. The dirt Paul tossed to one side became the Appalachian Mountains.

You may have heard that Paul made the Rocky Mountains that day, too. He could have, but he didn't. He made the Rockies another day. It happened when Hot Biscuit Slim made a batch of biscuits. Slim left them in the oven too long, and they came out hard as rocks. Paul almost cracked his teeth trying to eat one. He threw out the whole batch. They landed in a big pile, and that's what made the Rocky Mountains.

Paul's first camp was on the Onion River. The bunkhouse was so big the men had to have maps and compasses to get around. Even so, some of the loggers got lost. Paul had special searching parties on duty night and day to round them up. Most of them didn't stay lost for more than a week, but a few were never found.

When the loggers changed shifts, there was a real to-do. So many of them were coming and going that they got jammed up between the bunks. Paul fixed that in a hurry. He put up red and green stop-and-go lights, inventing the first traffic system.

The cookhouse, where the loggers ate, covered three or four square miles. Sometimes a man would faint with hunger while hiking to his table. Paul put in lunch counters along the walls. That way a man could have a bite to eat before starting on his regular meals.

The loggers' favorite food was hotcakes. Paul drained out a small lake near the kitchen, giving the cooks a place to mix the batter. An old steamboat was kept going around the lake. The paddlewheel stirred up the batter, better than anything else Paul could think of.

The griddle for the hotcakes was the biggest ever made, though Paul never did get around to measuring it. The griddle was round, and Paul just didn't have the time to invent a round measuring rule. Once, though, he stood at the edge of the griddle and whistled. Johnny Inkslinger figured that it took the whistle six minutes to travel all around the griddle and come back to where it could be heard. To grease the griddle, a couple dozen bull cooks would skate on it, with slabs of bacon tied to their feet.

When the hotcakes were done, they were loaded on a train that ran right to the tables. On the tables waiters rode bicycles up and down, serving the hotcakes to the men. The waiters didn't bother with the maple syrup. Paul ran that through a pipeline, direct from New England. The loggers could shove their plates under the pipe and get all the maple syrup they wanted.

Paul ate as many hotcakes as anyone else, and maybe more. What he really liked, though, was corn on the cob. Once he tried planting some. He only planted one stalk of corn, but that was enough. It grew so fast the top went clean out of sight. Hals Halvorsen tried to climb up to pick a few ears for Paul's dinner. When he was half way up, he saw he'd never make it to the top. He tried to slide back down, but he couldn't. The cornstalk was growing as fast as he could slide, and he was getting nowhere fast.

This went on for two or three days, and Paul couldn't help laughing. And that made Hals' temper boil.

"Yumpin' Yimminy!" Hals said. "Here I am, stuck up here. Maybe I'll be here the rest of my life. Maybe I'll starve to death. And you yust laugh! By Yimminy, Paul, to me it's not funny!"

Paul hadn't meant anything by laughing, of course. He was the biggest hearted fellow you could hope to

meet. He saw that things were serious, so he hollered up to Hals:

"Keep slidin', Hals! I'll get you down, one way or another! I'll get you somethin' to eat, too!"

Paul loaded his big shotgun with some of Hot Biscuit Slim's biscuits. He aimed at Hals, shooting the biscuits up to him. While Hals ate, Paul ordered his axmen to chop down the cornstalk. The axmen did their best, but it wasn't any use. The cornstalk grew so fast their axes never made a dent in the same place twice.

Paul thought about it for a minute. Then he ripped up some rails from the logging railroad. Making a cable out of the rails, he tied it around the cornstalk. He made a good, tight knot, so that the cable wouldn't slip. The cornstalk was growing thicker as well as taller. As it kept growing, the cable cut into it. At last it cut itself in half and began to topple over. It fell for two days, raising a cyclone of wind.

When the cornstalk hit the ground, Hals jumped off.

"Welcome back, Hals," said Paul.

Turning to his men, Paul ordered them to pick up the ears of corn for a corn roast. Before they could do it, though, something happened. The weather suddenly turned hot—just why, nobody knew. Most likely, the cornstalk fell so fast it heated up the air.

Anyway, it got so hot the thermometer boiled up, melted, and blew off steam. And the corn started to pop. There was popcorn busting out on all sides, flying through the air like a snow storm. It piled up on the ground in big drifts. It covered the roof of the cookhouse and the bunkhouse. It stayed on the branches of trees. It looked just like snow, for a fact.

Flocks of birds headed south, thinking it was winter. Paul's mules fell over, stiff with frostbite. Paul's men shivered and shook. Even Babe the blue ox turned bluer with the cold.

"By the great horn spoon!" roared Paul. "Start eatin' this popcorn and get rid of it, before we all freeze to death!"

All of Paul's men started eating the popcorn. They munched and crunched and gulped and swallowed, until they could eat no more. But there was still plenty of popcorn on the ground.

Paul had been eating with the rest, and he was still going strong. But his arms were tired from picking up popcorn. So he lay down on his back, ordering his men to pour the stuff into his mouth with shovels. The men shoveled, and Paul ate, and at last the popcorn was gone.

The birds came flying back again. The mules stood up, and the men stopped shivering. Babe stopped turning bluer with the cold. Old Paul had fixed things again with his fast thinking. And yet he wasn't feeling the way he should.

"I'm kind of stuffed," he said. "Funny thing—eatin' sure spoils a man's appetite."

Paul was right, of course. For the first time in his life he couldn't finish his dinner. He ate a couple of bowls of pea soup, six steaks, a roast chicken or two, some mashed potatoes, squash, beans, a few stacks of hotcakes, a dozen doughnuts and an apple pie—and bread and butter with it all. But he had to push away his eighth cup of coffee. He just couldn't take another drop.

After that, Paul dug up the roots of the cornstalk. He sold them to the farmers of Iowa, who have been growing corn ever since. Paul was through with planting. He did raise a few lead pencil plants, so Johnny Inkslinger could have enough pencils for his rough figuring. And that was all. Paul tended to his logging, thinking up a lot of new wrinkles. The best of them was his grass-handled ax.

Paul's regular ax had a handle made of a hickory tree. Whenever he tried to do some really fast chopping, the handle would break. And even though the ax blade was seventeen feet across, it would only cut down one tree at a time.

It had Paul stumped for a while. Then he wove some tall grass into a rope about fifty feet long. At one end he made two handholds for his two hands. At the other end he fastened the blade of his ax. That way he could swing the ax around him in a big circle, chopping down twenty or more trees at one stroke.

Paul was so busy with his grass-handled ax, he didn't notice Hals Halverson shaking his head. To tell the truth, Hals kept shaking his head at anything Paul did. He just couldn't forget how Paul had laughed at him on the cornstalk. The more he thought about it, the less he liked having Paul for a boss. And that led to trouble when Paul started logging on the Upside-down Mountain.

The reason the Upside-down Mountain was given that name was that it was upside down. The peak was at the bottom, and the wide part was up in the air. Even the trees grew upside down. Paul saw right off that there was only one way to chop them down. The loggers would have to stand on their heads. It wouldn't be easy, but it could be done.

Hals Halverson shook his head. "Why not use the ho-dads?" he said.

Now the hodads were critters found all over the North Woods. They were especially thick, though, on Upside-down Mountain. They were built something like buffalos, weighing about three tons each. Hal's idea was to scare them so they wouldn't know whether they were coming or going. They'd crash into the trees, knocking them all down.

"It's a good idea, Hals," said Paul, "except for one thing."

"What's that?" Hals said.

"It won't work. Hodads just don't scare."

Paul was right, of course. The hodads were mighty ugly critters. If they weren't scared of each other, nothing could scare them—not even a logger.

But Hals was tired of being bossed by Paul. He took a running jump and leaped on the mountain.

"By Yumpin' Yimminy," he said, "we do it my way yust this once!"

"By Jumpin' Jehosophat, we won't!" roared Paul.

And he leaped to the mountain beside Hals.

The next minute, Paul and Hals rolled up their sleeves and started to fight. Hals was about as big as Paul, and about as strong. But Paul was a little faster on his feet. Even so, the fight went on for three days. The two rolled all over, grinding the mountain into dust. With no mountain to grow on, the trees just fell down. All the loggers had to do was haul them away.

When Paul saw what had happened, he said, "Look! What are we fightin' for?"

"By Yimminy, I don't know," said Hals.

They walked away, arm in arm, singing:

> *And once more a-lumbering go,*
> *And once more a-lumbering go.*
> *And we'll range the wildwoods over,*
> *And once more a-lumbering go.*

That was the last time Paul and Hals fought. They were together on many a big job, and never a cross word between them. One of their biggest jobs was logging off North Dakota. It seemed that more and more people were coming to the United States, filling it up. They needed land for farming, and Paul figured North Dakota would be a good spot. That is, it would be, once the forest was cleared. Paul set up camp in North Dakota and started to work.

Cutting down the trees didn't give him any trouble. But it did leave the ground covered with stumps. Paul fixed that, too. He and Hals walked all over the state, knocking in the stumps with their fists. When they finished, North Dakota was as nice a place to farm as you could find.

From North Dakota, Paul and his men went to Wisconsin. And that's where Paul ran into the Howlin' Round River—or the Round Howlin' River, as it's sometimes called. Paul didn't know it was either one when he started logging. He set up camp, the way he always did, and everything went along fine.

The weather was good that winter. Once there was a storm of blue snow, but it didn't harm anybody. Anyway, Paul fixed things in a hurry. He took Babe and hauled in some white snow from China. It was in December, and Paul wanted a white Christmas. Any other time, he wouldn't have bothered.

There was one pretty cold spell. Whenever a logger talked, the words froze as they hit the air. Paul's frozen words were put in a bucket. They had to be thawed out on the bunkhouse stove before the men could hear his orders.

Still, it wasn't what anybody would call a hard winter. In the spring, Paul floated the logs down the river, taking them to the saw mill. And then something funny happened. Paul passed a camp that looked just like his own. The bunkhouse, the cookhouse, even the hotcake griddle were as big as Paul's.

"Somebody's been stealin' your ideas," Johnny Inkslinger said.

Paul just laughed.

"I don't mind," he said. "I've got plenty more."

The next day, Paul passed another camp that looked like his.

"Somebody else has been stealin' your ideas," Johnny Inkslinger said.

Paul smiled.

"Let 'em," he said. "I've got more than I can use."

The day after that, they passed a third camp that looked just like Paul's.

"I guess everybody is stealin' your ideas, Paul," Johnny Inkslinger said.

This time Paul didn't laugh or smile.

"By Jumpin' Jehosophat!" he said. "This is goin' too

far! I'm a good-hearted man, but too much is enough!"

Jumping to the shore, Paul ran up to the bunkhouse. There he stopped, not knowing what to say. For this was Paul's own camp, that he'd left three days ago. He'd passed it twice, and come back to where he started. Something was wrong.

Paul thought for a minute, pulling at his beard.

"The way I figure it," he said, "we must have been on a round river. It's got no beginning and no end. We've been riding around in circles, passing our own camp each time."

Johnny Inkslinger was standing beside Paul. He did some quick figuring on a piece of paper, and tears came to his eyes.

"Twenty-seven million feet of lumber!" he said. "That's what we cut. And now we can't get it to a saw mill. Paul, this is going to bust us."

"Oh, I don't know," said Paul. "We've been in tough spots before. The trouble here is that we've got a river with no beginnin' and no end. All we've got to do is build a beginnin'—the end will take care of itself."

And he gave Sourdough Sam orders to mix the biggest batch of sourdough that was ever mixed. Paul's men thought he was out of his mind.

"This is no time to be eatin'," they said. "Paul, you've got to think up some way to get those logs out."

Paul made out he didn't hear them. He had them mix the sourdough in the big pot the cooks used for making pea soup. There was too much of it for Sourdough to mix alone. The men stirred it with shovels and poles, while Paul himself kept dumping in sacks of flour.

When the sourdough was ready, Paul hitched up Babe, his blue ox. Pulling the big pot to the river, Paul dumped the sourdough right in. The stuff began to swell and harden, making a fine dam. The water rose over the banks and started to flow away. It wasn't a round river any more.

"That does it," said Paul. "Now that the circle's broken, the river's got a beginnin'. Where it will end I don't know, but it's bound to pass a sawmill sooner or later."

The men raised a cheer, watching the water rush along. And then from the river came the most awful howl that had ever been howled. It sounded like a thousand timber wolves, mixed up with buzz saws and the northeast wind. On top of that, the river reared up in a big wave, dousing Paul with several hundred gallons of water. It took Paul a full day to wring his beard dry.

At first, Paul just laughed it off.

"Take a river that's used to goin' around all the time," he said, "she's bound to do a little howlin' when she's turned loose. It won't last."

But this time Paul was wrong. The river kept on howling, once every half hour. With every howl, it reared up and splashed water. There was no way of driving logs down a river like that. Paul had to think of something, or he'd be stuck with twenty-seven million feet of lumber.

Paul had himself a good look at the river, sighting along it as far as he could see.

"That's it!" he said. "I should have known! No wonder the river howls. She's full of kinks and twists and curleycues. You'd howl, too, if you were in such bad shape."

"What are you going to do, Paul?" Johnny Inkslinger asked.

"Don't know yet," said Paul. "I'll have to think."

And he began to think, fast and furious. When Paul thought like that, his head always got hot from his brain working so hard. Sometimes his hair would start blazing away like a forest fire. To play safe, Paul usually lined up his men in a bucket brigade. They'd toss water on his head, to keep him cool.

But Paul hated to let anything go to waste. He sat down on the river bank to do his thinking. Every time the river reared up, it gave Paul a good wet. He could have done with a bit less water, and the howling bothered him some. Still, he didn't mind going to a bit of trouble, if it meant not wasting something.

A great cloud of steam rose from Paul at every splash. He'd take a deep breath and blow the cloud away. He blew so hard the steam went clear across the Atlantic Ocean, making a fog that settled down on the British Isles. In fact, that same fog is being used in London to this day.

Well, Paul sat there thinking for quite a spell. He held a pine tree in his hand, combing stray drops of water out of his beard. Suddenly he stood up.

"Boys," he said, "get me a long length of chain. Get me Babe, my blue ox. Then stand back, for I aim to straighten out this river good and proper."

Paul wrapped one end of the chain around the river about forty-eleven times. He looped the other end around Babe, his blue ox.

"All right, Babe," he said. "Pull! Pull away! Heave!"

Babe braced himself and pulled. The strain was so great that the big ox sank six feet into solid rock. The chain stretched until it looked as though it would bust.

The river howled and splashed, carrying on something fearful. Babe bellowed. Paul roared out his orders. His men yelled, cheering him on. And yet, with all that noise, the river didn't budge.

Then Paul took hold of the chain himself, standing beside Babe.

"Altogether now, Babe!" he said. "Pull! Pull away! Pu-u-u-u-ull!"

That did it. There was a loud noise, like thunder coming over the mountain. The river gave one long splash. It gave one long howl. And after that, it was quiet evermore. For its kinks and twists and curleycues were gone. For miles and miles it ran, as straight as a ruler.

Of course, the river was a lot longer, now that it was straightened out. Even so, Paul had a big pile of little bits and pieces left over. Anybody else would have just thrown them away. Not Paul, though. He had his men roll them up neatly and tie them with bailing wire. He sold them to farmers in dry country, who used the pieces of river to wet their fields.

With the river so quiet, it didn't need its howl, either. Paul cut it up into slices, selling them to steamship companies. They were used in foghorns, one slice to a horn.

Yes, Paul hated waste—and that's why he hasn't been logging for some time. What happened was this. Whenever Sourdough Sam made hotcakes, there was always a stack or two left over. Johnny Inkslinger tried to figure out how many hotcakes should be made every day, but it couldn't be done. Some days a man would eat a hundred. The next day he might not be hungry, and would eat only ninety-five. And since there were at least seven hundred men in camp, it added up to a sizeable stack or two every day.

Paul couldn't stand throwing them out, so he fed them to Babe, his blue ox. Now hotcakes aren't a natural food for an ox. Everybody knows that. But Babe learned to like them, and wouldn't eat anything else. To tell the truth, he just couldn't get enough. He'd hang around the cookshack for hours, pestering the cooks. Sourdough Sam complained, and Paul chained Babe to a mountain.

Soon as Paul's back was turned, Babe yanked at the chain. He couldn't break one of Paul's chains, of course— but he pulled the top of the mountain right off. He sneaked over to the cookshack, where he saw some pancakes sitting on the stove. Babe didn't bother with syrup or butter or any fixings. He just opened his big mouth and swallowed the pancakes, red-hot stove and all.

Smoke and flames shot out of Babe's mouth, lighting up the countryside for miles around. Roaring and bellowing, Babe lit out for the North Pole. He figured that the only thing that could cool off the hot stove was drinking the cold water of the Arctic Ocean.

Paul ran after him, of course, all the way to the Pole. They're still up there, with Babe standing in the cold water, lapping it up by the gallon. And that's why Paul hasn't been logging for a long while. He's waiting for Babe to cool off.

Some loggers say that swallowing the stove was the end of Babe. They say that Babe exploded, blowing into bits. Well, some loggers will say anything, just to make a good story. The fact is that the winters aren't as cold as they used to be. That's sure proof that Paul and Babe are still up in the Arctic. For something is warming up the winters at the North Pole, right where they're made. And what else could it be except the hot stove in Babe's insides?

One of these days, though, the stove will cool off, and Paul and Babe will go back to logging. And when they do, there will be big doings again in the North Woods. By Jumping Jehosophat, it will be just like old times!

John Henry

JOHN HENRY was born way down south. Yes, down south in the cotton country, where the Mississippi flows. And yet he wasn't a cotton-picker in the fields. Nor yet was he a roustabout, rolling bales of cotton on the steamboats.

Oh, he could pick cotton, and he could roust cotton. He could, better than the best. But he was meant to drive steel on the railroad, because he was a natural man. Yes, yes, he was a natural man.

John Henry knew what he was meant for. He knew, even when he was a little baby. Sitting on his pappy's knee, he said:

"I'm goin' to drive steel. Goin' to whop it on down with a big hammer. And that hammer will be the death of me. Yes, that hammer will be the death of me."

John Henry's pappy smiled.

"Son, you're just makin' foolish talk," he said.

But John Henry's mama looked at John Henry. She gave him a long, slow look. His skin was as dark as deep night, and his eyes shone like two bright stars.

"I'm a natural man," he said. "And I'm a steel-drivin' man. And I'll die with my hammer in my hand."

John Henry's mama made up her mind he wouldn't. She wouldn't allow John Henry to end his days that way.

97

She would raise him so he wouldn't go to driving steel. She would take care that he never held a hammer in his hand.

John Henry's mama didn't let on what she was thinking. But anything she made up her mind to, she did. Instead of going out to pick cotton, she took in washing from the white folks. She tied John Henry to her apron strings. She kept him close to her side. She watched him and looked after him. And he never held a hammer in his hand.

Then one day John Henry's pappy was picking on the banjo. John Henry took the banjo from his pappy's hands. He picked out a tune, the same as his pappy. He really made that banjo ring.

"That's it! That's surely it!" said John Henry's mama.

"What's it?" said his pappy.

"That's what the boy's going to be," his mama said. "A music man. And then he'll never hold a hammer in his hand."

"Music man," said John Henry's pappy. "Well, he could try."

Going out of the cabin, he hitched his mule to the wagon. He and John Henry's mama got on the seat, with John Henry between. And they took John Henry to New Orleans, to the professor on Perdido Street.

Soon as he was in the professor's house, John Henry ran to the piano. He played that piano, the black and white keys, both. He didn't miss a one.

"Child," said the professor, "you can sure tickle them ivories. Where did you learn to play like that?"

"It just come to me natural," John Henry said. "Because I'm a natural man."

Then John Henry beat out a roll on the professor's drums. He played the drums fast time, slow time, double time, ragtime, and no time. Then he picked up the slide trambone. He played it sweet and he played it low. Then he picked up the clarinet. He played it hot as fire and cool as ice. And then he picked up the trumpet. He made it laugh and cry, snicker and sob. Why, he almost made that horn talk.

Folks crowded around the door, listening.

"Play it, boy," they said. "Play it!"

And John Henry played. He played everything from *Mushrat Ramble* to *High Society*, and plenty in between. The professor picked up the slide trambone and joined in. Somebody took the drums, and somebody else the clarinet. From the house next door a man brought a bass horn. Folks came running from everywhere, singing and clapping hands. They followed John Henry down the street, dancing, marching, high-stepping. John Henry blew glory on his trumpet, while the folks sang:

Oh, when the saints,
Oh, when the saints,
Oh, when the saints go marchin' in,
I want to be in that number,
When the saints go marchin' in.

"That's surely it," said John Henry's mama. "John Henry is goin' to be a music man."

But it didn't turn out that way. Because John Henry was growing, faster than any weed. He grew until he was eight feet tall, and he was still growing. There wasn't a trumpet or a trambone made to match his size. And John Henry was strong. He didn't dare put a finger on a piano, or beat a drum. He would just smash and crash them to bits.

"Well, you can sing, maybe," his mama told him.

"I beg to differ, mama," said John Henry. "I can't sing, unless it's outdoors and far from a house. For every time I let loose with a song, it raises the roof."

To show his mama, he sang out "Mi, mi, mi, mi!" And the roof raised.

"Well, then," his mama said, "you can just stay home, the way you've been. No need to trouble yourself about anything."

John Henry shook his head. "No, mama, I don't mean to cross you, but I can't stay home. Not with pappy's back bent from pickin' the cotton, and you worn and weary from washin' the clothes."

"I'm not lettin' you go to work on the railroad," John Henry's mama said. "I'm not lettin' you drive steel with a hammer in your hand."

"I could pick the cotton. That wouldn't do any harm," said John Henry.

His mama thought, "No. It might not do harm. But do you pick cotton, you'll see the roustabouts on the river. And you'll want to roust cotton. And do you roust cotton, you'll see the steel-drivin' men drivin' steel on the railroad. And you'll want to drive steel. And do you drive steel, you'll die with your hammer in your hand."

That's what John Henry's mama thought. But she didn't let on. She knew she couldn't hold John Henry back. Couldn't anybody hold him back, because he was a natural man. Yes, yes, he was a natural man.

And so John Henry went to picking cotton in the fields.

His pappy and his mama went with him. At first they were faster than John Henry. He picked cotton and put it in his sack, picked cotton, put it in his sack. After a while, though, John Henry's hands moved like lightning. It was pick and put, pick and put, pick and put. And while he worked, he sang:

> *You got to jump down, turn around,*
> *Pick a bale of cotton,*
> *You got to jump down, turn around,*
> *To pick a bale a day.*

John Henry picked more than a bale a day—lots more. From sun-up to sun-down—from can-see to can't-see— he worked in the fields. It was pick cotton the livelong day, until all the crop was picked.

It was time, then, to take the bales of cotton to town. Time for the roustabouts to roll the bales aboard the steamboats. They dug their hooks into the cotton, taking the bales up the gangplank. John Henry watched them. While he did, a white man eyed him every which way.

He was the captain of the roustabouts, that white man was.

He said, "Where you come from, boy? How did you get so big?"

"It just come natural, cap'n," said John Henry. "Because I'm a natural man."

"Boy, think you can roust cotton?" asked the captain.

"Think I could, cap'n," John Henry said.

The captain handed him a cotton-hook, and John Henry rousted that cotton. Soon he was rousting cotton every day, just as his mama feared. At first he used one hook, and then he used two. Sometimes he carried a bale or two on his head, besides. He rousted more cotton than any ten men, piling it up on the steamboats. Folks came from miles around just to see the sight.

Among the folks was a pretty little girl by the name of Polly Ann. She liked John Henry and John Henry liked her. They kept company for a while. Then they were married, setting up housekeeping in New Orleans. Polly Ann was a good wife. When John Henry came home from his work, she had his supper waiting. There was side meat and corn pone, turnip greens and black-eyed peas. Or there might be chicken and biscuits and maybe pot licker. Even John Henry's mama couldn't do better than that.

With a wife to keep, John Henry rousted more cotton than ever. But one day he passed a place where the railroad was being built. He saw a crew putting down the wooden ties, and the rails on the ties. He saw the gandy dancers, packing down the crushed stone. And he saw the steel drivers, driving in spikes with big hammers.

John Henry had picked the cotton, and rousted the cotton. He'd done both, better than the best. But he knew now he'd only been biding his time.

"Cap'n," he said to the captain, "could I heft one of those hammers? Just to sort of get the feel."

The captain gave him a hammer to heft.

"Cap'n," he said to the captain, "could I drive in one of those spikes? Just to sort of see if I can."

The captain gave him a spike to drive. John Henry raised the hammer, and it made a rainbow around his shoulder. He brought the hammer down, and there was an awful rumbling sound. He hit the spike and whopped that steel on down. Yes, yes, he whopped that steel on down.

"Boy," said the captain, "where did you learn to drive steel like that?"

"Never had to learn, cap'n," said John Henry. "It just come natural. Because I'm a natural man."

John Henry hefted the hammer again.

"Cap'n," he said, "you got a job of work for me?"

The captain said, "Boy, you're workin' now. I hired you two minutes ago. Now line out those rails! Let me see you whop that steel on down!"

And so John Henry went to driving steel. He had a hammer in his hands at last. It came about just the way his mama feared. The tears sprang to her eyes when she heard the news.

"I tried to hold you back, John Henry," she said. "I tried and I tried. But couldn't anybody keep the hammer from your hand. And that hammer will be the death of you."

"Now who told you that, mama?" John Henry asked, though he remembered.

"You did. When you were a little baby, sittin' on your pappy's knee."

"A little baby don't know," said Polly Ann. "A baby says anything comes into its little head."

"Why, sure," said John Henry's pappy. "Just fool talk. I said it then, and I say it now. No cause to fret."

"Maybe," said John Henry's mama. "Maybe so. I hope, I hope and I pray. But I won't try to stop you, son, because I can't."

After that, John Henry drove steel every day. At first he used one hammer, and then he used two—one in each hand. Sometimes the railroad men couldn't wait until all the track was laid. It didn't worry John Henry any. He'd run out on the ties, with a train chug-chugging right behind him. He'd have his two hammers, and a mouthful of spikes. He'd spit out the spikes and drive 'em in, keeping just ahead of the train. When all the track was fixed, he'd jump aside, and the train would rush on.

John Henry traveled around some himself. He worked in eastern Virginia and western Virginia. He did the same in Georgia, Alabama, and Mississippi, too. Not that he had an itch in his heel. Oh, no, he wasn't the rambling kind. But he was a steel-driving fool. Wherever track was laid, John Henry was wanted. The captain told him to go, and he went.

So John Henry wasn't surprised when he was sent to western Virginia again. This time his job was a little different. A tunnel had to be built, to get the C. & O. Railroad through a stone mountain. To make the tunnel, dynamite had to be used. To use the dynamite, holes had to made in the rock. The dynamite would be dropped in the holes, and *blam-te-blam!* it would blow up the stone on the mountain. John Henry's job was to make the holes in the rock, driving in a big steel drill. The drill would be held by a man called a shaker, while John Henry whopped it on down.

John Henry took Polly Ann with him to western Virginia. She was a big help. Whenever John Henry was sick and took to his bed, Polly drove steel like a man. Yes, yes, Polly drove steel like a man.

It didn't happen often, though. John Henry was strong, and he wasn't sick more than once or twice. From the dark of morn to the dark of night he drove steel on the mountain. Then he hurried home to Polly Ann. They had a little son now, and John Henry liked to hold him on his knee. The little tyke would grab John Henry's big finger in his little fist. He'd hold on and he wouldn't let go.

"I do declare," said John Henry. "This baby got a power of strength. He's goin' to be a natural man, and a steel drivin' man, just like his pappy."

Some days Polly Ann would take the baby and bring a lunch to John Henry on the mountain. She was there when the stranger came around, with his fast talk and his fancy clothes. He carried a strange contraption, and was looking for the captain.

"What's that you've got there?" asked the captain.

"Glad you asked," the stranger said. "For I'm here to tell you. And you'll be happy I did. For never, sir, have you seen the like. It's the marvel of the age. It's what you've been needing. It's what you've been wanting. It's what you must have. Try it, sir, and you'll say the same."

"I might. And then again I might not."

"You will, sir!" the stranger said. "You'll see, sir! It's bound to please. And to amaze and astound you as well."

"But what is it?" the captain said.

"Aha," said the stranger. "I was coming to that. I was, indeed. This, sir—" and he waved his hand— "this is a steam drill. It does the work of three men in half the time."

"I don't need it, then," the captain said. "I don't want it. I don't have to have it. Because I've got a boy here does the work of six men in hardly no time at all. Name of John Henry. He can beat any machine that ever was."

The stranger threw back his head and laughed. He laughed and he laughed.

"Know when John Henry will beat this steam drill?" he said. "When the rocks on this mountain turn to gold."

The captain turned to John Henry.

"You hear that, John Henry?" he said.

"I hear it, cap'n," said John Henry. "I hear the words, but I don't hear the sense. Cap'n, a man ain't nothin' but a man. But before I'd let that steam drill beat me down, I'd die with my hammer in my hand."

"Huh! No man can beat a machine," the stranger said.

"He can if he's a natural man," John Henry said.

The stranger wasn't laughing now. He looked mean.

"Uppity, ain't he?" he said to the captain. "Talks big. Acts big. Mighty biggety and uppity. But I've got just the thing to put him in his place." He patted the steam drill with one hand. "How about a race, sir? My steam drill against John Henry. I'll give you a steam drill, free and for nothing, if John Henry can beat it down."

"And what if he can't?"

"Then you'll buy a steam drill from me."

"You hear that, boy?" the captain said to John Henry. "What do you say?"

"Don't you do it, John Henry! You got no call to beat a steam drill!" Polly Ann said.

It was John Henry's turn to laugh.

"Cap'n," he said, "I'll beat that steam drill to the bottom, or I'll die."

"Good boy," the captain said. He told the stranger, "You've got yourself a race. Week from today suit you?"

"Suits me fine," the stranger answered.

And, shaking hands with the captain, he took his leave.

All that week folks kept coming from everywhere, to see the race. John Henry's mama came, and his pappy. His mama was afraid. And this time his pappy and Polly Ann were afraid, too.

"John Henry," said his mama, "you goin' to die with your hammer in your hand. You said so yourself."

"That was just fool talk," John Henry said. "When I was a little baby, and didn't know A from izzard."

"I'm not so sure," said his pappy.

"I've been driving steel some time," John Henry said. "And I'm still here. Still alive and kickin'."

"Now see here, John Henry," Polly Ann said. "You never raced a steam drill before. Don't do it, John Henry."

"Don't do it, son," said his mama and his pappy.

"Why, I couldn't back out now," John Henry said. "Not with all the folks here to see me. Besides, the cap'n wouldn't like it. And all the drivers and shakers would laugh. So stop your frettin' and your fussin'. Little ol' steam drill can't do me any harm."

John Henry wouldn't talk about it any more. He laughed, and ate good, and played with his little son. The morning of the race, he joked while they walked up the mountain. When they reached the top, he waved his hand to the crowd.

"How you feelin' boy?" the captain asked him.

"Feelin' mighty spry," said John Henry.

The sun was coming up over the mountain, blazing hot. Not a breeze of air stirred. John Henry took off his shirt and picked up his hammer. He lifted it a few times, just to limber up his muscle. The crowd cheered, and he looked around.

There was his shaker, holding the steel drill. There was the steam drill, with the stranger beside it. There was the crowd watching, and the captain. There was his mama. There was his pappy, and Polly Ann holding his little son. And there was the mayor of the town in his high hat, his gold watch and chain in his hand.

"Ready with the steam drill, sir?" the mayor asked the stranger.

"More than ready," the stranger said.

"You ready, boy?" the mayor asked John Henry.

"Yes, sir," John Henry said.

The mayor looked down at his gold watch and chain.

"Then go!" he said.

John Henry raised his hammer, and the ground shook underfoot.

"The mountain's sinkin' in!" the stranger cried.

"Why, that's just my hammer suckin' wind," John Henry said.

The crowd laughed and cheered.

"That's it, boy!" they said. "Whop that steel, John Henry! Beat that steam drill down!"

And John Henry drove steel—wham! wham! wham! And the steam drill hissed and drove steel—bam! bam! bam! The race was on. It was the machine against John Henry, and John Henry was a man. Yes, yes, he was a natural man.

His hammer flashed like lightning, as he sang:

> *There ain't no hammer,*
> *Upon this mountain,*
> *Ring-a like mine, boys,*
> *Ring-a like mine!*

The drill cut into the rock, and John Henry sang to his shaker:

> *Shaker, why don't you sing?*
> *I'm throwin' twelve pounds*
> *from my hips on down,*
> *Just listen to the cold steel ring,*
> *Just listen to the cold steel ring!*

John Henry kept bringing his hammer down, faster and faster. Then, after a while, his hammer wasn't so fast any more. But still he kept driving steel. Near him, the steam drill kept turning. And the sun went high in the sky, and the sun went low in the sky. And the steam drill kept turning, and John Henry kept whopping that steel on down.

Then the sun went down behind the mountain, and the mayor looked at his gold watch and chain.

"Stop!" he said. "I declare this race over."

He counted the holes John Henry had drilled, and the holes the steam drill had drilled. He measured to see how deep they were, every one. He cleared his throat, took off his high hat, and said: "John Henry's drilled more holes! And he's drilled them deeper. I declare John Henry the winner. He's beat the steam drill down!"

Well, the crowd cheered. Well, they stomped and yelled and carried on. John Henry smiled, but he didn't smile for long. He pressed his hand to his heart, and he laid him on the ground.

"Where's my mama?" he said. "Where's my pappy? Where's my sweet Polly Ann? And where's my son?"

They all gathered round him, and Polly put John Henry's son in the palm of his hand. John Henry held him up. The little tyke reached for the evening star, as if he could pluck it from the sky.

"You got a power of strength in you," John Henry said. "A power of strength."

He gave his son back to Polly Ann. Then a trembling came over him, and the mountain shook. And he died with his hammer in his hand—died with his hammer in his hand.

Well, they took and buried John Henry. And every time the people passed his grave, they said, "There was a natural man. Yes, yes, John Henry was a natural man."

Joe Magarac the Steel Man

THAT Joe Magarac—he was one good man for making steel! Nobody in the U.S.A. could make steel like him, and nobody in the whole world, or in the Monongahela valley, even. Ho, he was one good man!

A funny thing, though—the first time anybody saw Joe Magarac was at Steve Mestrovich's party. And who was Steve Mestrovich? If you listen, you will hear.

Long, long ago, Steve lived in the Monongahela valley, in a town near Pittsburgh, Pennsylvania, U.S.A. He was a Slovak fellow, with a big mustache. Like the other Slovak fellows, Steve worked in the steel mill. When he wasn't working, he was in his little house, way up on a hill. Looking down, he could see the mill near the river. All day, the smokestacks blew out smoke. All night, the fires of the furnaces lit up the sky.

"By golly," Steve said, "that is nice picture for my eyes. It means they are making plenty good steel."

Sometimes there was a noise from the mill—like everybody throwing pots and pans.

"By golly," Steve said, "that is music for my ears. It means the mill is working good."

Next to making steel, Steve liked his missus and his

111

daughter, Mary. Steve's missus was the best cook around. His daughter was the prettiest girl around. She had nice yellow hair, nice blue eyes, nice pink cheeks. Every young fellow in the mill wanted to marry her. Mary liked Pete Pussick best, but Steve wouldn't let her get married.

"Mary," he said, "you are prettiest girl around. You have to catch hoosband that is best and strongest man around. You just wait a while."

Then, one night, Steve was smoking his pipe in the kitchen. He sat by the window, looking out at the fire of the mill. His missus was baking a cake, and Mary was sewing a new dress.

Pretty soon, Mary said, "That Pete Pussick is a fine fellow."

"Oh, a fine fellow," said Steve's missus.

"Sure, sure," said Steve.

Mary said, "Pete has good job in the mill."

"Oh, a fine job," said Steve's missus.

"Sure, sure," said Steve.

Mary said, "He will make some girl a good hoosband."

"Maybe some girl," Steve said. "But he is not hoosband for you!"

Mary began to cry. "Hoo, hoo, hoo! Every time I talk about Pete, you are making holler on me!"

"I'm not making holler just for holler!" Steve hollered. "I want you should have good hoosband! Now don't cry!"

And he banged his fist on the table—boom!

Steve's missus screamed. She took the cake out of the oven and held it under Steve's nose.

"Look, Mr. Steve Mestrovich!" she said. "You make bang on table, you make my cake fall in! All my work for nothing!" And she started to cry, "Hoo, hoo, hoo!"

Steve put his hands to his ears.

"Stop!" he said. "Better you broke my head with a rolling pin! But I can't stand for to hear womans cry!"

Mary and Steve's missus looked at each other. They each gave a little wink, but Steve didn't see. Then they cried louder than before: "HOO! HOO! HOO!"

"Don't cry!" Steve yelled. "Listen! I have good idea. We will have party this Sunday. We will invite Pete Pussick, Eli Stanoski—all young fellows that want to marry Mary. Then we will find out who is best man for hoosband. All right?"

"How will you find out?" said Mary. And she and Steve's missus cried again, "HOO! HOO! HOO!"

"I will bring dolly bars from mill," Steve said. "Big hunks steel—heavy like anything. The man that can lift up those dolly bars must be strong man. Whoever does it will be hoosband for Mary."

"Ho!" said Mary. "Pete Pussick is strong man. He will pick up those dolly bars and be hoosband for me."

Right away, she and Steve's missus stopped crying. They smiled and winked at each other.

And so Steve and his missus and Mary got ready for the party. They made cakes and plenty good things to eat and drink. Steve got the gypsy band from Braddock to play music. And he invited everybody to the party, especially the young fellows.

On Sunday, a big crowd came to the party. Fellows came from everywhere—from Homestead and Braddock, from Monessen and Duquesne, from McKeesport and Port Perry, from Johnstown, even. They all had nice barber haircuts and wore their Sunday suits. Girls were there, too, dressed in pretty dresses. In the yard behind Steve's house were tables loaded with good things to eat and drink. The Gypsies played their fiddles. The fellows and girls danced polkas, and everybody had a good time.

Then Steve stood up on a box so everybody could see him.

"All right, everybody!" he said. "I am glad you come to my party. I am glad you eat and drink good things, made by my missus, best cook around. I am glad you dance the polka. But that is not why I give party. Oh, no. I give party because I want to find best hoosband for my daughter Mary, prettiest girl around."

He pointed to the three dolly bars, on the ground in front of him.

He said, "Anybody wants to marry my daughter Mary, he will try to lift those dolly bars. The first one is a little one, weighs only three hundred pounds. The next one is heavier, weighs five hundred pounds. And the big one weighs more as the other two put together—maybe a thousand pounds. Any man can lift that, he is one strong fellow, by golly! He will be Mary's hoosband for sure! Now stand back, everybody, and we start!"

The crowd stood back in a circle, and a lot of young fellows stepped up. They took off their coats. They rolled up their sleeves. Every one of them tried to lift the first dolly

bar. But only Pete Pussick, Eli Stanoski, and a man from Johnstown could do it.

Then Pete and Eli and the Johnstown man tried to lift the second dolly bar. Pete and Eli could do it, but the Johnstown man gave up.

"Yay!" yelled the crowd. "Now pick up the big one, Pete! I'm for you," and "Eli! You got plenty steam!"

While the crowd was yelling, Pete and Eli took off their shirts.

"You want to try first?" said Pete.

"Sure," Eli said. "You can't lift that big dolly bar anyhow. You just move away, little boy, and a man will show you how."

"Where is the man?" Pete said.

"Here. Me," said Eli, making big muscles in his arms. He leaned over, took a grip on the dolly bar, and pulled.

Nothing happened. He pulled harder—and fell on his face. Everybody laughed, Pete Pussick most of all.

"Move over, big man," he said. "Give me plenty room to lift up this dolly bar."

Eli moved over, shaking his head. Pete rubbed some dirt on his hands. He put his feet wide apart, leaned down, and took hold of the dolly bar. He gave a big pull, and one end lifted up just a little bit from the ground. It didn't lift high—just enough so a fly could crawl under, maybe. Then Pete's hand slipped, and he fell back on the ground.

Before Pete could stand up, somebody in the crowd laughed, "Ha, ha, ha!"

Pete yelled, "Who is making laugh? You are such a smarty Alex, why don't you pick up this dolly bar? You try it, you gone broke your back! That shut up your mouth, I betcha!"

"O.K.!" a voice said. "I try. But my back don't broke so easy."

Then a man stepped out from the back of the crowd.

"Ho-o-o!" said everybody, but not loud—more like a whisper.

Because that man was the biggest man ever seen in the Monongahela valley. He was almost as tall as the tree in Steve Mestrovich's yard. His arms and legs were thick as telephone poles. His hands were as big as shovels. And he was so wide, he looked as though he couldn't get through the gate in the steel mill fence.

Everybody was looking at him, but he didn't look at anybody. He just picked up Pete Pussick with one hand. With the other hand, he picked up the dolly bar. He lifted them high over his head, gave them a shake, and put Pete back on the ground. Holding the dolly bar in his two hands, he twisted it like a pretzel.

"Yay," said the crowd, again like a whisper.

Everybody started to move back, even Eli Stanoski and

Pete Pussick. But Steve Mestrovich walked up to the big man.

"Hey!" said Pete. "I don't invite you to my party. Who are you?"

The big man looked down at Steve.

"I am Joe Magarac," he said.

And when he said that, everybody started laughing like anything. Because in the Slovak language, magarac means jackass donkey.

"Ho!" said Steve. "That is some name! Joe Jackass Donkey!"

"You betcha!" Joe Magarac said. "I am magarac for sure! I work all the same like jackass donkey."

Everybody laughed some more, and Joe Magarac laughed with them.

"Where do you come from, Joe?" asked Steve.

"I was born on ore mountain in Old Country," Joe Magarac said. "But now I am come here to make steel. I am real steel man—only one in the U.S.A., or the whole world, or the Monongahela valley, even! Look, I show you!"

He opened up his shirt—and he was made of shiny steel all over.

"By golly, he is a steel man for sure!" said everybody. They crowded around, touching Joe Magarac's steel muscles, looking him over. All of a sudden, Steve slapped his own head.

"Yoh!" he said. "I almost forget why I give this party! Joe Magarac, you picked up the dolly bar. You are best and strongest man around. You will make good hoosband for my daughter Mary."

Joe Magarac smiled at Mary, raising his cap.

He said, "Oh, my, you are pretty girl! You are more pretty as any girl I ever see. But I got no time to be hoosband. I have to make steel, day and night. I am real magarac, and I work and eat like magarac, and that's all. Better you marry Pete Pussick. Next to me, he is best and strongest man in Monongahela valley."

Mary and Pete Pussick both got red in the face, like the red stripes in the U.S.A. flag.

"O.K.!" Steve said. "We will have the wedding right now."

He sent for the priest and the altar boy, and right away Mary and Pete were married. Joe Magarac danced with the bride, while the Gypsy band played music. Then everybody danced polkas, ate cakes and drank good things, and had a nice time.

Early the next day, Steve took Joe Magarac to the steel mill. The foreman gave Joe Magarac a job on Number Seven furnace in the open hearth. When he started to work, everybody came running to see him. Even the big boss superintendent came in his high hat and long-tail coat.

Because that Joe Magarac, he didn't need any helpers. He threw limestone, scrap iron, and ore into the furnace. While it was melting, he sat in the furnace door. The

fire shot up all around him, and the foreman yelled: "Hey! Look out, you!"

Joe Magarac laughed and said, "Don't you worry for me, boss! This fire don't make no never-mind to Joe Magarac!"

After the fire was melted down, Joe Magarac put his big hands in the furnace. He stirred the hot steel around and around. He took a little taste of it, and said:

"Mmmm! Pretty soon this steel be cooked up good, you betcha!"

When the steel was ready, he dumped it in the ingot molds. But he didn't take the molds away to be rolled into rails. Picking up handfuls of steel, he squeezed out rails between his fingers. He made eight rails at a time, each A Number 1 perfect. Oh, he was one good man for making steel!

After that, Joe worked all day in the steel mill. When night came, he kept right on working. He worked day-turn and night-turn, not even stopping to sleep. He didn't rent a room, but he ate five meals a day at Mrs. Horkey's boarding house. When anybody asked him where he lived, he said:

"In steel mill! That is the home of Joe Magarac!"

For a long time Joe worked, making plenty of good steel. Then one day the foreman walked up to him.

"Joe," the foreman said, "the mill is going to shut down for a while. You put a slow heat in the furnace, so it will keep warm until we'll be ready to start up again."

Joe Magarac laughed.

"That is good joke, boss," he said. "Steel mill never shut down."

"It's no joke," the foreman said. "Maybe we will be shut down only a few days. Maybe a few weeks. Maybe a few months."

"But why?" Joe Magarac asked.

"I don't know. But big boss super say shut down, and we shut down. That's all I know."

Joe Magarac shook his head, but he did what the fore-man told him to do. Then he patted the furnace with one hand.

"Goom-by, old Noomber Seven," he said. "I hope I will see you soon."

Slowly Joe Magarac left the mill. He walked up the hill where Steve Mestrovich had his house. Standing on top of the hill, he looked down into the valley. No smoke was coming from the smokestacks. There was no big noise, like people throwing pots and pans. It was so quiet, he could hear the whistle of a bird flying past.

"Ho, little bird," he said. "Fly away home. You got nice nest to go to. But where can I go? My only home is steel mill—and that is shut down."

After watching the bird fly away, he went into Steve Mestrovich's house. In the kitchen were Steve and his missus, and Pete Pussick and Mary.

"Hello, everybody," Joe Magarac said. "Say, Steve, maybe you know how come mill is shut down."

"Just hard times, I guess," said Steve.

"But what everybody gone do?" Joe Magarac said. "If mill is shut down, nobody get paydays. Nobody have money for eat, for pay rent, for buy clothes!"

While he was talking, a little fellow named Frank Olinsky walked in. Frank worked in the drafting office. He wore a blue suit, white collar, shined-up shoes, every-thing nice.

"I hear you ask how come mill is shut down," he said. "I will tell you how come. Big boss super wants to build fine new steel mill, best anyplace. But he has to have right kind of steel for beams in new mill. Engineers can't figure out how to make it. Until they do, mill will be shut down. That is how come."

"Big boss super wants best steel for new mill?" said Joe Magarac. "Engineers don't know how to make?"

"That is right," said Frank.

"By golly!" said Joe Magarac, a big smile on his face. Jumping up, he ran to the door.

"Where do you go, Joe?" Steve asked.

Joe Magarac winked one eye. He tapped a finger against the side of his nose. "I go to front office! I tell big boss super how to make best steel in world! Then mill won't be shut down, you betcha!"

"You crazy in the head, Joe?" Frank Olinsky said. "You will tell big boss super how to make steel? You will tell big college engineers?"

"Sure, I tell anybody. Maybe some day they do me a favor, too," said Joe Magarac.

"But guards will not let you in front office," Steve said. "And in the second place, big boss super will not listen to you in the first place."

"He will listen to me any place," said Joe Magarac.

And turning around, he ran out. Steve and Frank Olinsky and Pete Pussick ran after him.

"Joe!" they said. "Wait! Don't go, Joe! You will get in big trooble!"

They tried to hold Joe Magarac back, but they couldn't. All the way down the hill, they hung on to him. They saw some fellows from the mill, and called to them.

"Help!" hollered Steve. "Hold back Joe, before he gets in big trooble!"

More fellows tried to hold Joe Magarac back. Soon, by golly, a whole crowd was hanging on to him. But Joe just kept on walking. When he reached the mill, the guards closed the big gate in his face.

"Ho, ho!" said Joe Magarac. "Little gate can't stop big steel man!"

He put out his big hands, and bang! bang! he knocked

down the gate. He pushed away the guards and the crowd of fellows. He pushed away more guards at the door to the front office. Throwing open the door, he walked right in. The big boss super was there, and the big engineers. They were sitting around a big table, smoking cigars.

Before they could say anything, Steve Mestrovich came running in.

"Excuse, boss," he said. "Joe don't mean to make trooble. Don't throw him in lock-up. He will go away."

"You don't listen to Steve, boss," Joe Magarac said. "You listen to me. I will tell you how to make best steel in world for new mill. Then everybody will go to work again, you bet."

"You will tell me how to make steel?" the big boss super said. "And you will tell all these engineers?"

"Where did you learn to make steel? Where did you go to school?" the engineers asked.

"I don't go to school," said Joe Magarac. "Just work in mill, that's all."

Throwing back his head, the big boss super started to laugh. The engineers threw back their heads and laughed, too. Even Joe Magarac laughed—a little bit, to be polite.

"Now we have nice laugh," he said, "I will tell you how to make that steel."

The big boss super laughed harder than ever, and so did the engineers. Oh, they made some big laugh at Joe Magarac.

Steve pulled at Joe Magarac's sleeve.

"Come on, Joe," he said. "Better you go now."

All of a sudden, Joe Magarac gave a holler, louder than the twelve o'clock whistle on the mill. He pushed away Steve Mestrovich. Outside the door, he knocked the heads of the guards together. And then he ran.

"Stop him!" yelled the big boss super. "Throw him in the lock-up!"

So the guards and everybody looked for Joe Magarac. Steve and the big boss super and the engineers looked all over the mill. But they couldn't find Joe Magarac anywhere.

But as they passed by Number Seven furnace, Steve and the big boss super heard something:

"Ho, ho! Hoo, hoo, hoo!"

"What is that?" said Steve.

"Who is that?" said the big boss super.

"Is me!" said a voice. "In ladle!"

Steve and big boss super looked in the ladle—and there was Joe Magarac. He was sitting in the hot steel. It was boiling up all around him, steaming and bubbling.

"Get out of that ladle!" said the big boss super.

"Hurry up! You are steel man—you will be melted yourself!" said Steve.

"Sure I will melt," said Joe Magarac. "That is what I want. By golly, I can't sit around waiting for mill to open again! Maybe those engineers never find the right kind steel to build new mill! So I start up furnace. Now I melt myself down, and it make best steel in world for new mill, you betcha! You take this steel with me inside, you pour 'em out, you roll 'em into beams and everything for new mill.''

Everybody came running up, looking at Joe Magarac in the ladle. All they could see was his face.

"Get out, Joe!" they said. "Don't do it!"

"Too late," said Joe Magarac. "Goom-by!"

Then the hot steel in the ladle went bubble, bubble, bubble—and Joe Magarac was all melted down.

"Goom-by, Joe," said Steve Mestrovich. He took off his hat, and the other fellows did the same.

For a while, nobody moved or said anything. Only the hot steel in the ladle bubbled and hissed.

"All right!" hollered the big boss super at last. "Don't just stand there! Pour out that steel! Roll it into beams! That's what Joe Magarac wanted, by golly, and we'll do it!"

Everybody jumped to do what the big boss super said. They poured out the steel with Joe Magarac in it. They rolled it into beams and girders. And they made the biggest and best steel mill in the world, with plenty of smoke, and fire that lights up the sky, and a big, big noise like a crowd of people throwing pots and pans all over the place.

Ever since that time, if you call a man in the mill a magarac, he will just smile.

"You don't make me mad, sport," he will say. "Because you don't mean me—you mean Joe Magarac. He was real magarac, all right." He will take off his hat, and point to the beams and girders. And he will say, "Good old Joe Magarac. He is still inside those beams and girders, best steel in the world for best steel mill anywhere."

And, by golly, you better take off your hat for Joe Magarac, too—because he was sure as anything one good man for making steel.

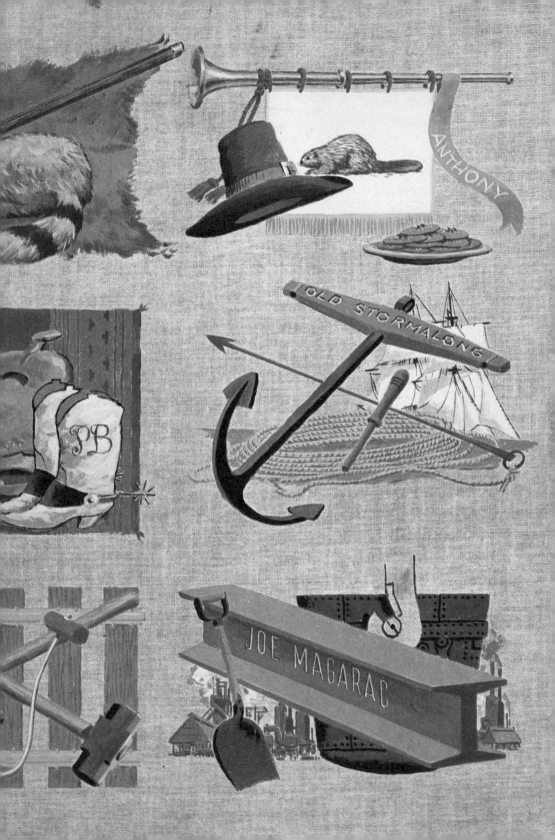